WARNING: Disclosure Statement

Due to the graphic nature of this program, viewer discretion is advised. This work is not intended to offend any nation, race, or other differences a person can have. ***READ AT YOUR OWN RISK***. Please control your emotions/thoughts so you can receive all the information. This book is for entertainment **AND** educational purposes. It would not hurt to grab a pad and pencil so you can take notes. Do not forget, ignorance kills all opportunities for advancement.......

The Midnight Mirage Presents...

"Keep It Black and White"

Author: Chaz Norfleet

The Midnight Mirage Presents...

"Keep It Black and White"

Author: Chaz Norfleet

The Midnight Mirage Inc. Book Publishing
Atlanta, Georgia

THE MIDNIGHT MIRAGE PRESENTS
"Keep It Black and White"

Published by:
The Midnight Mirage Inc. Book Publishing
Atlanta, Georgia
chazn25@yahoo.com
Chaz Norfleet, Publisher / Editorial Director
Yvonne Rose/Quality Press, Production Coordinator
Printed Page, Cover & Text Layout

ALL RIGHTS RESERVED

No part of this book may be reproduced or transmitted in any form or by any means – electronic or mechanical, including photocopying, recording or by any information storage and retrieved system without written permission from the author.

The publication is designed to provide accurate and authoritative information in regard to the subject matter covered. It is sold with the understanding that the Publisher is not engaged in rendering legal or other professional services. If legal advice or other expert assistance is required, the services of a competent professional person should be sought.

Midnight Mirage Books are available at special discounts for bulk purchases, sales promotions, fund raising or educational purposes.

© Copyright 2014 by Chaz Norfleet
ISBN: 978-0-9906690-0-5
Library of Congress Control Number: 2014914218

Dedication

To Grandma and the Armour Clan

The Midnight Mirage Presents...

Acknowledgements

I first want to thank my mom for giving me the original inspiration to be a creative thinker and go beyond the box. Next, I want to thank my bro and sisters for love when I was down. Next, I want to thank my dad for showing me the value of self-knowledge.

Salute to Bobby Hemmitt, Phil Valentine, Professor Griff, Dr. Umar Johnson, and Sara Suten Seti for dropping real wisdom. The information helped me tremendously during my spiritual graduation phases. Thank you to every teacher that ever taught me. I was very fortunate to have good teachers outside of my home.

Thank you to every random person I ever got light from. Throughout my life, I always had people around who talked positive. Thank you to the great mother for birthing my unstoppable soul. Thank you to Yvonne Rose who helped me materialize my spiritual excursions. You will never know the ultimate justice you have established. Last but not least, I thank all the readers and dreamers of the Midnight Mirage. I am happy you have chosen to take your life to the next level and graduate. You are the reason this book exist.

The Midnight Mirage Presents...

Contents

Dedication	vii
Acknowledgements	ix
Preface – "The Midnight Mirage"	1
Section One: The Old Testimony	7
The Primordial Point, 000	9
Tamahu Terror	12
Hibernation, ZZZZ	16
Aiwass's Anarchy	20
Wisdoms of Tehuti	23
Sobek and the Underground Railroad	25
Akasha's Aftermath	27
Children of the Baphomet	29
Choices	31
Hazel and the Wands of Horus	33
Separate and Beyond Equal	35
Free at Last?	36
Intermission – Breathe First	39
Section Two: The New Testimony	41
Ch1 – The Black Dot	43
Ch2 – Misery in Malkuth	51
Ch3 – Kali's Crossroads	57
Ch4 – Heart Ascension	67
Ch5 – Rise of the Khutis	81
Ch6 – Kether's Kiss	89
Ch7 – Fireside Chat	95
Epilogue – Lyrics to Go	103
Bibliography / Resources	105
Shout Outz	107
About the Author	109

The Midnight Mirage Presents...

Preface:
"The Midnight Mirage"

Right now, your mind is twirling and swirling towards the door of another dimension. You have been traveling for some odd or even number of years, approaching a distant division hidden in your subconscious. Prepare your brain to experience new phenomenon and many unidentified flying thoughts. The key to the door in front of you is ***your own mental art form***. The possibilities are endless and your momentum will determine your progress. Brace yourself as you enter the mysterious maze of mystique. Many will start, few will finish. Be my guest, as we pioneer to the west. Welcome to the house of hallucinating horrors, better known as the **Midnight Mirage**.....

    The laws of thermodynamics state that energy cannot be created or destroyed, but can be transferred from one place to another and one type to another. The peculiarity behind energy is the apparent intelligence it possesses. Let's take the universe for example. Fundamental constants, such as the gravitational field, remain on duty as if on a payroll. Why hasn't it collapsed? Or the perfect relationship the power of the Sun has with the requirements of Earth's needs. Stars like Sirius could leave Earth fried. How did that work out?

    What about the photon theory of light? We know light carries discrete particles called photons. Sunlight grows plants and supports everything we know of. Obviously, this light is carrying "information" to hosts and is conscious of what gets which type of light. Could there then be a "photosynthesis" of a human being? What if light could transform *you*? We all know the physical body is a reflection of the atomic structure that makes it up. So essentially, the human body is **non-physical**. You know, protons and neutrons. But what exactly is an electron? We arrogantly use these words as if we are 100% sure this is what it is. Could the atoms be forms of *light*?

Science has shown us electrons orbit around the nucleus of atoms. There are different types of atoms so there have to be different levels of energy, right? Or wrong? And what is sound? Is it another form of the same light? We know sound waves come in different frequencies. How does it travel in the wavelengths? How come it never breaks? Must we add the human brain? What an entity. The master composer of the physical matrix. Think about your eyesight. Did you know your brain receives the visual information **before** your eyes? Crazy, right?

This is why sometimes we will see blue instead of red. Ever notice how people say, "My bad, I **thought** I heard you call my name." Why didn't your ears tell your brain what was heard? Why does the brain have the final say so on all of the senses? Is the brain on our side? Is the brain always in your **best** interest? Dopamine and adrenaline is pumped to save you from "fear or danger". But this same mechanism could cause you to respond to something absurdly. If you have ever over or under estimated anything, you have experienced this brain betrayal before. This chaos carnival goes on in your head non-stop.

Think about yoga. You probably pictured a person sitting and meditating. But what are they *really* doing? Are they trying to wake up their inner atoms? Are they talking to themselves? Are they crazy? Life has also revealed the human body has an outer energy field. Ancient people left knowledge describing a holographic universe. In other words, dimensions are stacked on top of each other as a reflection of the less dense form. Remember how your eyesight works. What you see is a reflection of what the *brain* says. So the brain controls the image. Same with the cosmos. The above spectacle determines and dictates this mundane reflection.

Are you connected to the outer you? Who really runs your life? We all know of the *doppelganger effect*. Have you ever been riding and something will tell you to turn down another street. And this could be a street you are unfamiliar with and never take. As you drive, you soon realize there was an accident on the other road. Weird. And we all have that "voice" in our head. Who actually is this voice? It sure seems to know a lot about you. Do you have a twin? Is this how you knew to pick your phone up before it rang? Or is it the "devil"?

We all know the voice sure does like to challenge things. It will always make you go to a level you did not think you would go to. Isn't it strange how in the Bible the devil always is the one to ignite the change in people's lives? At first it seems like it hurts but we all have said that cliché phrase, "What doesn't kill you makes you stronger". Which is very true. So in essence, did the devil actually help you? And what about this birth to "mankind"?

We are told Adam and Eve. Or is it the evolution from primate? Challenging isn't it? Many never stop to think about some of the information they have been living off of. Is this actually your information? Or did someone program it into you? What about your thoughts? Are you actually using your own thoughts? Yes, tonight we are going deep folks. Your whole life, other people have been tugging and pulling for your attention. Charming you for a hidden reason. Showering you with fruit from the tree of ulterior motives.

Regardless of what we want to think, the average person never develops into who they truly are. We live in a society of clones. Androids. Humanoids. Two-legged sheep. Everyone's mind follows the same pattern. Eat, work, sleep. Monday thru Friday. Saturday we gorge ourselves with blasphemous alleviators and Sunday we ask Jesus to forgive us. Does Jesus hear you? Is he even there? Who said Jesus was a man? What if God has a mom? If most of us began to answer these questions, many would give the exact same answers. The Sesame Street, good-ole American answers. And there is nothing wrong with that if you first know **truth**. What is truth? Well, that's where the indigo cloud gets thick.

You see, there is no universal truth yet universal truth concepts are jammed down our ears daily. For example, treat a person as the way you want to be treated. The golden rule, right? Well what about racism? Do you actually think a racist person wants to be treated that same way? Probably not. They want to treat someone cruel and have that person treat them nicely. We say all people walking this Earth are the same. That we are all one big Earth family. But is this true? Do we act like it is true?

Many think racism doesn't exist today. Does it? We allegedly live in a de-segregated country. But do we really? What is a class system then? An aristocracy? Don't we live in an economically segregated world? Or are we all the same financially? Is the phenomenon of a "middle class" even real? Could it just be the high end of the lower economic class? Where did money come from? Who created it? We are told it serves as a "legal tender". Well what is a legal tender? We know that we have multiples of financial instruments/assets in the world. Is money just one version of a legal tender? Could the required legal tender change? Baffling, I know.

When we pull back Van Allen's belt, we find a lot. Without the truth, you are nothing more than a floating leaf in a fall wind. You have no power. You are vulnerable. Your back is open. You may be wondering what the real point of this book is going to be. The point will be what you make it. ***Picture it like a vending machine, what your imagination puts into it, your reality receives***. Living in modern times is a tough cookie. We all know this. And we all attempt to solve this problem, typically, the same way.

We work harder for some financial gain that will purchase us wonderful items one day. Items for escapism and gratification. But are you truly satisfied? Could you go a day without your cell phone? Can you sit in a room for 24 hours with no physical stimuli? Are you "cool" with yourself? Who is your real "bff"? Can you stand yourself enough to be alone? In the darkness? Do you think your friends are really your friends? What is a friend? How does it feel when you hear the skeletons in your closet clawing at the door? Are they there? Have you cleaned them out?

Does nature agree with you? Will the squirrel run in the road to die for you? To wake you up? Are you sleep? Do you know what being sleep really is? Where do you think the disappearing aircrafts are going? Space? The bottom of the ocean? Another dimension? Where is Amelia Earhart? What do you care about? Are you gentle? Are you kind? What do people say about you when you are not around? Would you be embarrassed if God sat in the back of your classroom? What would you do if God called time out? Deep in your mind would you have any doubts? Are you gonna run? Try to hide, scream, and shout? Are you gonna drop to ya knees, cry and pout? What you gonna do when God calls time out?

Are you ready for the neo-mental apocalypse? Do you think weapons will always work? Can a bazooka shoot a ghost? Are you a ghost? Difficult, I know. Use this book to unleash your imaginary inner fairy. View the story as you are the characters, going through the journey. Because you will soon realize you are the character. The protagonist in your very own hero's escapade. Surely you have wondered why certain things have happened to you in your life. Things you can't explain. Some of them even hurt from time to time.

Tonight's episode involves a person very much like yourself. Someone who wondered and slumbered on the common questions of life. Yet again, a person you see in the mirror. Place yourself in the shoes of your neighbor. This is the moment that you become the NEW YOU. No longer are you relying on the world to show you how to be you. You are your own boss. You are your own thinker. You are the master of your cranial assets. Picture yourself as Superman/Superwoman. Batman/Batwoman.

Could your life tests be nothing more than a grueling process of human photosynthesis? Think of a period when your back was against the wall. Now think about all the hard times you overcame. Curious, isn't it? You always seem to make it out. Like Hercules fighting the Cerberus. Somehow you rose through the flames. How? Are you fighting dragons and saving villages in your sleep? Did you come from a planet of superheroes? Are you even human? Are you like Clark Kent? Posing as a teacher, lawyer, or plumber? Did you come flying out the black hole to save Earth? Outlandish, I know. I know. Or is it?

Relax your mind for the duration of this book. You need a clear state to fully understand its contents. This story is about you in some sort of way. Only you can figure out how. From time to time, we all must sit and ask ourselves. Does life imitate art, or is art imitating life? Do you imitate Cat woman or is Cat woman imitating you? No matter what the questions are, we all have them. We all ponder somehow and some way in our very own Midnight Mirage.....

The Midnight Mirage Presents…

Section One:
The Old Testimony

The Midnight Mirage Presents…

The Primordial Point, 000

Prior to the beginning, infinite pandemonium occupies all formless avenues of space. Energies move rapidly within cosmic placenta, having no order whatsoever. In addition, stellar glitches and malfunctions swirl amongst the madness. The central womb, full of pure love, emotionally tries to balance it all out. Unfathomable consciousness toils in the northern region, focusing on an immaculate conception. From the south gate, seas of starry, black milk funnel into existence. This would be known as the first "creation".

Seven cognitive stars follow the astronomical soup, separating from the flood. First, the mother, or "cow", star goddess stations near the opening, galactic urethra. Second, the daughter, or "emerald" star, comes. Third, the son, or "wolf" star falls in line. Fourth, the daughter, or "dove" star enters life. Fifth and sixth are twin "hawk" and "raven" stars. Seventh, at last, is the mercury daughter, or "death" star.

All the stars enjoy bliss in cosmopolitan heaven. The great mother watches her kids carefully, for she knows somewhere a flaw exists. One evening, the emerald star decided to go for a swim. As she swivels about, protons and neutrons bind together, resulting in dynamic types of energy. Whewwwwww!!!!!! The emerald star blows dark, violet purple clouds to absolve the alchemy. Baryonic materials collide, formulating meteorites, junior stars, and colossal asteroids.

The project expands for immeasurable distance. Like her mother, the emerald star was overrun by potent feminine passions. BOOOMMM!!! The emerald star manifests a customized, environment-friendly planet in her image. Duo hydrogen atomics marry oxygen solos, birthing liquid, clear life for Planet Earth. An immense, rocky supercontinent grows from the Earth's core. Healthy, green vegetation sprouts from under Earth's surfaces, introducing trees and landscaping.

The emerald star's biotechnologies produce animals and wildlife of all kinds. Whewwwww!!!! Spiritual winds wake Planet Earth's heart. Boiling inner astral elixirs shoot up Planet Earth's spine. She is now awake. Land and water mammals party on Planet Earth. Reptiles, insects, and birds inhabit the fields in harmony. Hue-stars, or hue souls, are blessed with a world of their own, living in prestigious paradise.

Rivers alternate between organic coffees, fruit juices, and wines at all times. Gardens harvest acres and acres of delightful foods. Caves of gold, diamond and various jewels fill the land. Hue women and men bond as **one ion**. Hue children play with the animals in the jungles during morning and night. Hue people populate the **ENTIRE** supercontinent, spreading out from modern day Africa's regions. The primordial utopia was so holy that it still networked with heaven's vibratory rate.

This is literally an *invisible, metaphysical phenomenon*. Let's briefly examine the profile of the hue entity. Ancient Atlantis hue beings psychologically function as "spiritual" beings. There are no such things as "codes", "standards", or "moralities". Replicated from the cow star, hue souls automatically synchronize with all stations beaming from the cosmic placenta. They control Planet Earth's weather, temperatures, and **moods**.

Planet Earth and Hue souls are actually one. When one is in harm, security receptors alarm the other to assist. Nothing but peace moves within Earth's boundaries. *Remember, as above, so below. As within, so without.* Transportation pyramids act as "airports" to visit any jurisdiction of the supercontinent. The lives of hue-souls stay in fortune, so long as they please their awesome mother. Eons and eons of time pass.

In the galaxy, far away, one of the junior stars grumbles and complains, **saturated in ego**. Enviously, the ego, or "vampire", star spies on Earth's joyous hue-stars. The vampire star is very jealous of his older, superior family. He was conceived *after* the implosion of the emerald star's procreation. Made from inferior particles, the vampire star struggles to shine like the others. Confused by ego, hatred builds in him, causing him to bully the cosmos habitat. The vampire star constantly is in search of a host, greedy for more illumination. He devours undeveloped stars, bloating himself with astral glutens. Back on Earth, mysteriously, things were changing. The vampire star's outer activities appear to be rearranging Planet Earth's polar fields.

Gradually but surely, Earth's gravitational and magnetic waves lose contact with high heaven's wave signals. The vibratory frequencies decline underneath the hue-people's awareness. ZZZZAAAAPPPP!!!! Atlantis is being covered by a physical shadow! All of Earth's belongings are materializing into tangible elements! Skin cells are surrounding hue-souls, capturing the floating freelancers. Spiritual genes code in constellation hieroglyphics, setting up DNA patterns for awaiting chromosomes.

The hue soul is now 100% **mummified**. Physical hue life resembles much of Ancient Atlantis, differing in the immortality department. Planet Earth reacts by adopting cyclical progression, or circumvolution. Planet Earth's seasons now govern natural law, obligating hue beings to adapt as well. Spring, summer, fall, and winter are born. Winter usually meant preparation or "re-alignment", while the subsequent seasons provide harvests.

Hue peoples establish academia, ranging from astrology to alchemy. Hue scientists constitute esoteric temples of learning to spread wisdom to all peoples of the world. Childhood and teenage years are spent investigating the laws of nature, climbing the ladder of knowledge. The top, ancient university mystery systems were located in what would be present day, central Africa. Hue beings physically advance as time elapses.

Planet Earth's giant supercontinent begins to crack among the edges. Sub-continents break away from the chunk of land, sailing miles away from the supreme slab. In the crevices, oceans flood Earth's gaps. Supercontinent becomes Ancient Pangea, slowly structuring the landscape. Ages and ages pass by. This winter, Planet Earth finds herself coming down with symptoms of the flu! Earth's temperature dramatically reduces, freezing water into continental ice sheets.

Outdoor movement starts to cease for hue beings, keeping them occupied indoors. Alpine glaciers coast on top of waters like frogs on lilies. The skies of ice storms release frozen thunderbolts and week-long blizzards. Hail drop sizes compare to small planets. Wide, gloomy clouds shade Earth from sunlight, while cosmic congestion clogs her sinuses. Lethargic and tired, Planet Earth presses on through the rough season....

Tamahu Terror

ZZZIINNGGG!!! Vampire star sinisterly grabs yet another innocent victim, withdrawing solar nutrients, puffing his ego. At present, ideas of adoration and kudos circulate vampire star's circumference, leading him to high levels of imperialist narcissism. Suddenly, uncomfortable convulsions erupt in his bowels. SPLASSSHHH!!! Scalding lava bursts apart in vampire star's small intestine zone of his south gate. Solar defecation mixes with pride, arrogance, and conceit. UGHHHH!!! Vampire star excretes feces throw up in Planet Earth's northward Alps.

The winter solstice comes to an end, rejuvenating Earth as well. Mystical potions heat Earth's liquid core, melting frozen snow across the globe. New valleys, rivers, and basins pour fresh water to support fertile, invigorating soil. Hue beings stretch in crisp air for the first time in months. Scholarship spirituality persists, moving up children to productive hue women and men. The Ice Age brought trials for a lot of hue people mentally. Frustration and lack of self-control drive some hue people insane.

Even certain wildlife died off. Planet Earth is in a new phase of animation, with different species and vibes. One odd life form yells loudly now in the northern hemisphere. Heathen, hairy, brutish, vulgar, red objects stampede in the Euro forests. These "red" beings, nomadic in nature, scavenge about in the brutally cold, windy parts of Earth. Red men search for food, only for the violent climates to shatter their chances.

In the woods, red men savagely fight each other for women and nutrition. Sizzling with testosterone, the red man expresses a bashful, blistering sexual psychology. Deep in the hills, sex between red women and men portray a fierce, homicidal, profane pornography. Impregnation and love thoughts have no mailbox in the red man's mind. Brisk nights send hypothermia and brittle fingers to the red man's body. Toes shatter like glass on the regular from frostbite. Starvation and malnourishment has the red man **crazed**. He develops pathology only he himself can justify.

The perception of the female counterpart creates puzzling enigmas for the red man. *She is good for the sexual pleasures her warm, wet sponge sacrifices to my bare member. But extra mouths are making things hard! I must figure out something!* thinks the red man to himself. Ding! Red men select a custom to kill excess female children and sodomize male boys. *The last piece of fish is mine!* thinks the red man. Red mothers, mind-bogglingly, accept their husbands' law. Young, red boys and girls are raped by the thousands.

As if on global intercom, red men in all places of Earth practice this same atrocity. How disturbing can this man get! But there is more. His father, the vampire star, blesses the red man for his grotesque methodologies, giving him insight to the vastness of Earth. "You can pay yourselves all the treasures of this land. I will give you the keys to wisdom, my sons! Obey my ego and you shall flourish!!" says the vampire star in the hearts of red men. With god on his side, the red man journeys his way out into the world. Hue people are appalled by the appearances of their new roommates. *Layers and layers and layers of dirt cover his skin. I would have thought he was like me, if not for his unique, crimson fur,* thinks a perplexed hue woman.

Showing compassion, hue beings accept some red peoples into their communities. Ancient hue Greeks and Etruscans show the red man how to bathe, reason, and other necessities. A variety of tongues and vernaculars are translated by hue priests for red people. Grunts and moans dominate his communication otherwise. Hue men teach him about existence, curiously striking the rookie learner.

Phoenician and Carthage masters educate the ignorant sub-being, boosting his small percentage of brain usage. Comprehension moves like a slug in the egomaniac's realm. Now somewhat sensible, red men start to conspire on Earth. Bloody conquest techniques dawn war after war for the red man. Collective narcissism segregates red societies, creating aristocratic members for red bureaucracy. Social governments, or "senates", oppress red citizens, leaving riches for the elite.

The Midnight Mirage Presents...

One summer night, a club of army red men rest after a long day of fighting. Servants are ordered to chef meals for the starving men. Kings of red empires enjoy fine, luscious wines and laughter throughout the night. Discussions come up about potential plans to colonize a near town. Conversations start regarding the building of state-of-the-art gymnasiums for the young boys. The men share cherished stories of unforgettable plunders. Next, the men dialogue about what a "honorable, red wife" is. The prince, Sextus, claims his wife is the epitome of dignity, submissiveness, and class. Red men argue versus Sextus, defending the loyalty depicted by their wives. "To justify our assertions, let's randomly peek on our spouses to observe them." says Sextus.

The drunken men saddle home. One by one, each red man bangs down the door of his house. Ashamed and embarrassed, most of the men found their wives mocking them, by indulging in recreational activities. Drinking and dancing to name a few. Yet, one wife embraces fashionable character. Lucretia was up late, spinning wool. She welcomes the men with refreshments. Lucretia's husband hysterically annoys Sextus with his win. When the night ends, all the men return to their respected homes. *How could Lucretia be guiltless! Surely she must be filthy!* thinks Sextus.

Weeks later, Sextus arrives to Lucretia's abode. "My husband is out for the day, prince Sextus." informs Lucretia. "I am weary Lucretia, may I have a drink of water?" inquires Sextus. Allowing Sextus' entrance, Lucretia steps backwards. Immediately, Sextus places a knife to Lucretia. "HELP!!" shouts Lucretia. Sextus rapes Lucretia like a dog, diving out the window afterwards. Hours later, Lucretia's husband returns home with a general named "Brutus". Depressed, Lucretia sits in the corner of the room. "Are you well, my dear?" asks Brutus. Lucretia weeps and explains the indecent act. Feeling unclean, Lucretia takes Brutus' dagger and stabs herself. "No!!!" screams Lucretia's husband.

Bring out the sword and armor. Scenarios such as this contaminate Earth with the irrational complex of the red specie. Red men entertain themselves with blood sports during free time. Coliseums hold chaotic, uncivilized, philistine ceremonies. Gladiators engage in sport-like battle, such as men fighting bears. Guts ooze out of victims, bringing red fans to a cheer. Red emperors demand to be treated as gods by all citizens. Non-believers are thrown to the lions and tigers of the arena. Original hue Christians are executed on the regular basis.

Martyrdom is prevalent, crucifying hundreds of Christian followers. Even red men and women die in name of the primitive faith. Father time continues to tick and tock. Red elitists instigate an economic system of suppression called "feudalism". Vassals seek the protection from Neanderthal savages ruling the wildernesses. Red elitists extort these poor red peoples, having them work field systems and perform other chores.

The partnership rewards big profits for the wealthy, leaving only pennies for the needy. Between revolts and enemies, life is becoming troublesome for the aggressive, red man. He needs a new lie to protect his stolen empire. Constantine, a Roman red man, enters the political ranks of war at a young age. In young adulthood, Constantine becomes a popular general, gaining ownership of red Roman territory in Britain, Gaul, and Spain. He values big dreams of one day controlling the entire empire.

While on political campaigns, Constantine realizes the abandoned red Christian district, causing him to wonder. Christian mercenaries pledge their allegiance to Constantine, adding to his military dominance. One night, Constantine lies down feasting on ideas on glory. The vampire star infiltrates Constantine's subconscious, showing him a sign of honor. The next day, Constantine and his infantry are seen wearing unfamiliar symbolism on their attire. Adversary armies perceive the Greek alphabet letters for "*Christos*" or "Christ". The vampire star allows salvation for the obedient Constantine, eventually crowning him sovereign king of Rome.

Constantine and the Christian regime achieve prime statuses. Favorable Christian laws are passed to arouse red Christianity. "New Rome" or Constantinople is founded, leaving only one last issue to solve. Now the red Christian has hijacked the religion from original hue peoples. Many of the traditions and requirements were too strict for the hoodlum red entity. A uniform, red Christianity must be made to accompany the authentic red man. The infamous "Council of Nicaea" held by Constantine and red priests solve the Christianity problem by indoctrinating the "stories of Jesus Christ".

The fairy tale of Jesus Christ gives credence to the red man to declare himself the "son of God". The vampire star's greatest illusion spreads like wildfire. Forged versions of Christianity are installed for red men of all parts of Earth. In the long run, Constantine's Holy Roman province collapses. Red Romans relinquish the land and spread out in Europe after the "Gothic Wars".

Vikings and Vandals tear down Rome's once beloved city. However, the red, Christian lords of Constantine's empire still direct Earth's path. Bans of homeless red peoples click together to help each other in these tough times. Anglo-Saxons settle in Britain, dictating under the factions of the "Kingdom of England". Germany, France, and Italy join the coalition, re-creating Rome's fragmented union. The "Holy Roman Empire" rises, in need of a new resource that will allow red men's covenant with mercantilism. The vampire star turns his attention to Africa's homelands….

Hibernation ZZZZ

Next, we will analyze the controversial, tragic crashing of the hue peoples. Incarnating to live on Earth is a harsh discipline one must remember for a liberal, free soul. Clairvoyance and other inexplicable abilities are traded for fleshly imprisonment. Homesickness plagues the hue beings, mentally forcing adaption to physical life. Not all hue beings are strong enough for the initiation. Aloofness and vanity smokes hue peoples' minds, opening their hearts for the parasitic vampire star. Hue men acknowledge their father, bowing down to his cunning ways.

To discern the red peoples' future influences, we have to see why hue spirituality ceases to exist. Let's launch from an estimation period of 100,000 years ago in Northern Africa/Middle East. **Please pay close attention to the following timeline**. Ancient Africa empires had full sovereignty across this mass region, classifying them as precursors to modern day Middle East/India. They are also the prototype Greeks, Etruscans/Romans, Phoenicians, and people of Carthage.

This Typhonian, or later named "Draconian", era venerate the great mother as a serpent called "Typhon" or "Apep". From a virgin birth, she has a son "Sut" or "Set". This ancient mythology predates all known to man.

As time goes on, *some* hue people incarcerate their own kinds, washing away all primitive spiritual bondages for the race as a whole. Typhonian beings develop into what we know as "Dynastic Egypt". Neophyte dynastic aristocracies bring forth a new political system, needing to convert old Typhonians to the current paradigm. Also recall, these are all the SAME groups of hues from the intro.

Desiring power, high priests decide to vilify the previous spiritual lens and re-model it for themselves. Familiar deities they use are Osiris, Amon Ra, Ra, and Ptah. However, Sut and Typhon's new role is one of the *antagonist* or *polar opposite*. Stories describe Sut doing villainous horrors such as murdering Osiris and bounding him to a coffin. Isis, or Osiris' other half, from a virgin birth, has Horus, to battle Sut's darkness.

For further clarity, do not forget hue beings were master astrologists. Most mythology is used to explain *astral phenomena*, not necessarily literal happenings. Anyhow, Ancient Egypt's dynasties alternate rulers from an assortment of hue families for centuries. Earth's cycles constantly revolve. Red men pillage Africa's continent, sending hue people into the jungles and inhumanity for the first time **EVER**. Red Greek and Roman scroungers colonize hue peoples and kidnap all hue scholarship.

Now, let's fast-forward to somewhere around 1000 BC. Akhenaten, an Egyptian pharaoh, upholds the political strategy of re-accessing previous gods/deities. He establishes Aten, the one, solar god. Strangely, all hue people end up idolizing "yesterday's god". Aten is none other than a re-telling of Amen. Akhenaten's dynasty declines as Africa is further molested by red men. Egypt's disciples morph into what we know of as the "Hebrews". Hebrew *religion* uses a lot of Egyptian spirituality, using hieroglyphic text translated by hue priests *before* Africa's cataclysm.

As centuries ascend, yet another new *religion* is birthed. A population of hue beings coin "Christianity", which is nothing but Hebrew-based faith. Islam and Judaism is put together this exact way as well. Here is where the red man makes his strike. After Constantine's inclusion of Christianity, red people campaign Earth to erase all pre-existing hue Christians. The Council of Nicaea conspiracy expedites their Jesus Christ cinema to the world. Once and for all, let's explore the ***true*** origins of Jesus Christ. Horus, in the Egyptian pantheon, assumes the character of the "light or Christ" energies. *Christos* is symbolism, not an actual last name.

After Osiris descends to Amenta, Horus tussles with Sut to ensure "lightness prevails over darkness". Alchemically, this is a formula representing "polarities" or twin forms of illumination. The physical incarnation of the hue soul is an example of the Horus and Sut myth. The light, or soul, struggles against the dark cloud, or human body. Horus is also recognized as "heru-khuti" or "Horus of the two horizons". In other words, "the rising sun in the east and the setting sun in the west".

Ancient spirituality was only for connecting back with the outer space worlds hue souls came from. Mythologies cleverly "*extrapolate inner phenomenon to analyze outer phenomenon*". Planet Earth is "Amenta", or the "underworld", that houses Osiris. As I said before, "As Above, So Below". Red priests simply fabricate Jesus by recycling the Horus myth. To throw salt on the wound, Jesus is also added to "real time history". Meaning Jesus is told as if he was a talking, live person like the one reading this sentence.

To speed up, let's compare Jesus and Horus myths: Horus of the two horizons (Twin Light and Dark Suns) to Jesus, the Christ (Jesus the earthly son and his twin soul), Isis, the virgin mother of Horus to Mary, the virgin mother of Jesus, Sut and Horus, twin opponents to Jesus and Satan, twin opponents.) Backing up, remember, ancient hue beings probably did not view "evil" as the way we do today.

At the Council of Nicaea, all the information red men could not understand was swept in a pile and labeled "evil". This was all the deep-rooted, spiritual essence of hue people's life. Satan, or the devil, is a very young concept also sculpted by red men. It is only a few hundred to a thousand years old. Christianity did not have the classical Satan until after the Council of Nicaea. He was made as a composite of multiple previous deities and **self-insecurities**.

Let's see who. The prefix, Sat, in Satan is derived from Sut and the suffix is from Anubis. Anubis is an Egyptian god who led you to the heaven realms and protects souls. So in conclusion, he is associated with the underworld or Amenta. Sut-An, or Satan, possesses qualities seen in other "horned-gods", such as Pan, the Greek goat, nature, god. Pan is described as a half-man/half-goat, found linked to sexuality too. Sat + Sut + Set = **Saturn**. Ancient hue astrologers explain Saturn's powerful magnetic tug with the use of these gods.

It was not evil, only energy released to re-order or re-align phenomenon. These deities also are copies of Capricorn, winter solstice principals. Hue beings prepare during winter's dark, cold months to re-train themselves for spring's blossom and fall's harvests. Ignorant red thieves mistake the formulas for wickedness, which occupies his own brain from his own hellish deeds. Red priests learn that these energies could blast them at any moment, causing chronic paranoia.

Red and hue people are mentally warped, taught that all the negative polarities are bad and hostile. Later day Christians demonize the well-known "Baphomet" drawn by Elipias Levi. Hue priests set up secret organizations to secure ancient, hue spirituality on Earth for good. Occultism is given to elite red men, through masonry and other secret societies.

During the Holy Crusades, hundreds of red members of the "Knights Templar" freemasonry are executed by the Pope's order for "devil worship and witchcraft". The Baphomet was the red man's tribute to his hue, Moor father, signifying the "completed hue man". This same Baphomet becomes present-day Christianity's arch nemesis, the devil, or Sabbotic goat. Now, instead of embracing responsibility, the world blames everything on the goat.

By the 19th century, Portuguese, Dutch, and British red men colonize the majority of Africa. Hue traitors, the first "Uncle Tom" or "House Negro", capture roaming hue people and sell them to red men. The feudal empire is about to take the ultimate conversion to outright financial gluttony. The souls of millions and millions of hue peoples go into hibernation. Ladies and gents, welcome to the "slave trade"....

The Midnight Mirage Presents…

Aiwass's Anarchy

Intersecting the treacherous African jungles, a union of hue beings prowl around in search of safe houses. Slave traffickers, both hue and red, prey on wanderers with high hopes of participating in trading for shiny prizes brought by merchants. Tired and hungry, these hue beings spot a small hut located up the road. Deceit!!!

A clan of hue beings lies in wait with red explorers, snatching up the vulnerable travelers. European red men often solicit help from native Africa's land to catch slaves, storing thousands of captives in dungeons up the coast. Hue people of the Eastern hemisphere get a first glance at their siblings, who speak different tongues. Voyages in the "Middle Passage" board hue-people, iron, ivory, cloth, brandy, and gun cargo for overseas investors.

Chained, naked hue beings frantically panic, unaware of what Euro-Red men's motives are. Thoughts of cannibalism infect their minds, putting fear in the hearts of millions. Cruel red men whip hue peoples over and over again. Women are heard squealing from being assaulted by lunatic predators. Oh how sad is this sight!! Kicked on to ships, the enslaved are met with red priests holding Bibles, sprinkling "holy" water, and chanting biblical parables. SLAM!!!! Hue folks are thrown to the ground, stacked like books on a shelf. Must I describe the smell? Sticky, hot climates bore the air, conjuring a toxic, foul odor. Concoctions of feces, vomit, and mildew inch its way into the lungs of victims. SPLASHHHH!!

Ill hue people are dumped into the ocean like waste. Many hue mothers commit suicide with their young. Contraptions expand open the mouths of demoralized hues, as red men shovel untasteful food substances down their throats. Some red men even kill each other, planning to cut into others' percentage of revenues. Be that as it may, not all hue men fall so easily. After months of sailing, red men grow impatient and lose focus. WHOOOOO!!! The howling, raining winds add spooky vibes this gloomy night.

While red men clean on top, one determined hue man stares at the moonlight from the basement. Stoic and wide eyed, Sengbe bobs his head in a trance. A small lady bug fairy flies into Sengbe's chains.

CLING!!! Sengbe's rusted handcuffs disintegrate, as other lady bugs do the same for other hue warriors. Sengbe and the hue men silently go up the basement steps, armed with boat tools. Let death's bell ring!! A hue female mermaid goddess creates a strong wave, rocking the red men and flooding the dock.

Frightened red men slip as hue warriors cogently charge. SINGGGG!! Sengbe's sword removes the head of a running red man. Hue warriors, robust in size, stab and stick weak red men. The red men are dying fast, unable to fight the hue man without firearms. In his peripheral, Sengbe sees a red man trying to hurt a hue woman. GUSSHHHH!! Sengbe's indestructible arm cracks through the red man's chest, pulling out his corrupt heart. Sengbe places the scared teenager on his back, leading her to safety. POWWW!!

A red man gets a hold of his pistol and shoots a hue man. Thunder rumbles!! As the red man reloads, he notices 7'0, 300 lb. Sengbe slowly approaching. The red man's inferior firearm jams as he refills gunpowder. His fate was left in Sengbe's wrath. CRAAACCCKK!! Sengbe twists the red man's neck 360 degrees in one second. Petrified, the three remaining red men huddle together in a corner. Sengbe's crushing footsteps and dripping blood through the dock floor wakes the sleeping prisoners. Sengbe walks over and vigorously slaps the man. POPPPP!!! Weaponless and timid, the red men plead for mercy. Sengbe scatters the captain's papers, searching for a map. "Home!!!!" yells Sengbe's deep voice. He throws the map at a red man, named Prescott.

Prescott mischievously grins to his red colleagues. He re-navigates the boat, aiming for the western hemisphere. Sengbe sits on the front dock all day. Uncomfortable with water direction, Sengbe is deeply concerned about Prescott's judgment. Just in case, Sengbe arms more hue warriors for emergency problems. He goes to the basement, desperately looking for his brother. Results sadden Sengbe, learning he was sick and tossed over to the sharks. "AWWWWWW!!" rages massive Sengbe. Muscles bulky and brawn, Sengbe stomps up the basement cellar. "Please, not me!!" cries Prescott.

Sengbe's hands clinch Prescott's throat with 8 tons of pressure. Breath divorces Prescott's lungs, smashing his neck tendons. Compact stress ruptures the inner arteries. Afraid, one of the remaining red men leaps in the ocean to the stalking great white sharks. "Home!!!" demands lion-voiced Sengbe. Absent of reinforcement, the red man fakes like he is checking the map and boat. Legs trembling, urine drips down his khakis.

Sengbe goes looking for Maya, the teenager. She is nursing a hue woman in pain. Sengbe brings over fresh water and fish. He orders a hue man to find a warm blanket. As the sun rose, the solo red man can see thick layers of dusty, crimson clay. SPLASH! America's east coast stirs glee as he swims to her shore. Water noise awakens Sengbe and the hue warriors. Sengbe signs the warriors to respond for war. He consoles Maya and the wailing women. Sengbe wipes Maya's tears, smiling and kissing her forehead. He hands her a lion-toothed necklace and points to her heart. Sengbe makes Maya the new leader and walks away.

Red men on the dock help the red man out of the water. He fights to catch his breath. "The niggers...they gone....crazy!" says the gasping man. One red man tries to pursue the boat, but is halted. "No, he will kill you!!!" warns the red man. The other man proudly frowns. "Boy ain't no nigger worth scared of, you stupid?!" states the man. Ego on high, the foolish man runs up to the boat entrance. Sengbe ducks down, grabbing him by the face. "Mmmmm!!" moans the man. Sengbe paces his clamp, squashing the man's cranium. Brain matter and juice squirt everywhere.

Motivated hue warriors holler as they scatter to the streets. Unprepared red sailors are met with redrum. A unit of red policeman gallop with weaponry to the scene. AMBUSH!! Hue warriors jump on the horses, killing red men in close combat. POW! BOOM! Red men shoot rifles and pistols, subtracting hue fighters. Shaq Sengbe dismisses red men by the dozen. Multiple die at once, by Sengbe's bare hands alone. Red men sprint off to recover. Sengbe calmly speed walks to a large platoon of policeman. BOOOOMMMM!! A canon is fired at skyscraper Sengbe, knocking him to the ground. Bloody and persistent, Sengbe raises his wobbly body to keep attacking.

Stunned and flabbergasted, the red men could not believe their eyes. The canon is reloaded. BBBOOOMMM!! Sengbe catches the cannonball, falling to the surface. More troops come in and dispense with the few warriors left. Finally, the chaos ends. When the smoke clears, the red men find all the chained hue people standing still on the beach. Quietly, the appalled yet upset, hue peoples watch the whole showdown. Shortly after, red investors come to collect their cargo.

Wisdoms of Tehuti

Before we proceed, reminisce on the progress of the Euro-red man, from ancient Greece/Rome to the Holy Roman Empire to the Kingdom of England. From Euro-Britain, a group of terrorist, untrusting red men rebel against the primitive red man tax customs. These traitors leave mother Britain, extorting and exterminating ancient hue people of North and South America. Spaniard red men had used Christianity to de-humanize hue America, satisfying him with slaves and gold. These would be the Olmec, Mayan, Aztec, and Native American hue peoples.

These terrorist red men colonize North America, with expectations of building a new home. Red Britain goes to war with Red America for bragging rights. In the end, the two lovers remarry, tag-teaming in the slave business. By now, free labor has made TRILLIONAIRES all through red Europe. New to the game, red Americans turn the brutality meter to its farthest point.

The slave trade is the sole source of ALL red American landscaping, economic, social, and any other development made by red men in North America. Trees and forestry cover the virgin land, using slave labor to solve all construction debts. Some hue men are even used for the blueprint of the country's constitution. Hues are given no credit, leaving all the majesty to red men. Red slave owners hard-heartedly, unsympathetically, uncaringly, subjugate with an iron bull whip.

A federal fugitive slave law is passed, meaning all runaway and loitering hues are to be enslaved at all cost. Federal red American government rejects all notions of hues being considered as a "human entity". The famous Dred Scott case decision decided that " ***ANY PERSONS OF AFRICAN DESCENT CANNOT BE, <u>NOR WERE EVER INTENDED TO BE</u>, CITIZENS UNDER THE UNITED STATES CONSTITUTION***. "

The Midnight Mirage Presents...

More and more international red men invest in the lucrative empire. Red class systems are based on acres and slaves owned. Poor red people are ignored and forgotten. Red Americans sit back, smoke cigars, sip fine brandy, and read papers as the scorching, blazing Georgia summers bake laboring slaves. Brainwashed hue men tote shotguns and whips to oversee his fellow kin. His payment usually is an apple core, leftover rice, and opportunities to sleep at his master's feet.

Once more, we have to intermission for a blast from the past. Christianity's Frankenstein, or Jesus Christ, rips all organic spiritual fibers of the hue man and woman. The messianic red image pollutes their conscious, keeping shackles and obedience in place. Slaving five days a week, hues are methodically brain-zapped on Saturdays and Sundays.

Hue men are forced to indulge cups of moonshine, or pure rubbing alcohol. Mentally paralyzed, he is taken to impregnate his woman. No love, compassion, or tenderness is shown during sex. Red man sex psychology hijacks the hue man's natural emotions. As a boy, hue men are often sodomized by homosexual slave masters. This diabolical procedure totally fractures the young boys' self-esteem. Now animalized, he is hurled into a horse stable, where he will live as beast. Now grown, the hue man is an uncivilized, untrained monster. Unprotected hue women are pitched to the hue stud, while he waits to sexually prance on his former queen.

On Sunday, slaves listen to red preachers inflate their heads with allegorical riddles told by Jesus Christ. The overwhelming desire for hope charms hues, allowing FrakenJesus to reach their souls. Maya lives on a large plantation on Georgia's coast. Teenage Maya dangerously sneaks books from the plantation, teaching herself academia. Maya would stay up long nights reading and writing. Weary from eye strain, Maya drifts away into a deep, peaceful sleep. A magical white and gold carpet scoops Maya, taking off to Earth's outer atmosphere. Mystical, illusionary designs gleam from the luminous angel carpet. WHOOOSHHH!! Maya and the carpet shoot blazing sparks behind them as they coast to the outer worlds.

Maya feels magnetic fields adjusting, pulling her away from Earth's mundane properties. Bells ring as her ears pop, while flickering, bright, rainbow lights flash before her eyes. Aero heat and cool winds penetrate her body, generating unusual sensations. After the long ride, Maya and the carpet land on a dark, crystalline, moon-like planet. Maya's eyes enlarge as she looks through the colorful spectrum prism ground. As Maya explores the magic carpet changes into two entities. One is a lioness-headed, dark hue-skinned goddess. She is with an ibis-headed, brown skin, hue man. "The soul can do wondrous things, innocent Maya," says the lioness goddess.

Maya studies the unfamiliar beings, mesmerized by their glowing, chocolate skin. "Maya, do you not know that Mother Earth is a mirror of yourself?" asks the ibis-headed man. Perplexed, Maya thinks for answers. "I do not know!" replies confused Maya. "You and the other captives of Earth are glorious gods, greater than ourselves." says the lioness goddess. Dazed and discombobulated, Maya sits on the rug to make sense of the complicating comments. "Alien foreigners were to fill the land and regions of Earth. Men of destitution, lacking an address, shall turn shrines and holy places into mausoleums and cemeteries.

Gore and irrationalism will outshine truth and righteousness. Commerce will replace intimate passions. Peoples of hue will be converted into clown, non-existent, automated, fiends. Life will be thought worthless, the pious will be seen as ludicrous, and the ancestors of the heavens will be ignored and banned. Natives will be suppressed and reduced by imposter strangers. And for all that, homeostasis will be restored by unique, exclusive divine beings of the western universe," concludes the ibis-headed man. Speculative of the statement, Maya opens her mouth to inquire. Unanticipated, Maya wakes from the dream in her usual state.

Sobek and the Underground Railroad

Since red America's commencement, the federal government has tried it's very best to avoid the slavery debates. Abolitionist hue and red people create major uproars about slavery's wrongfulness. The country is splitting, based only on domestic development, not actually slavery itself. President Lincoln even states if he could keep the country without freeing one hue, **he would**.

The Midnight Mirage Presents...

Northern red men stabilize themselves very minimally with slave labor, using industrialism to emerge the financial empire. Southern, Democrat red peoples live as cotton kings, viewing slavery as necessary and relevant. Political parties clash, irritating both red groups with the other's stubbornness. Georgia shows no sign of quitting slavery, clamping down even more on hue prisoners. As time moves on, southern states secede from the Union, founding the "Confederate States of America".

Once again, a group of red terrorists turn on their brothers. Economic advancement differences countdown to the first gunshots of the red American Civil War. America's east coast rumbles with Union and Confederate contests. The Union rejects hue soldiers while the Confederates force hue soldiers to fight. One fall, a Union campaign storms through Georgia, burning the state up. Hue slave men use this chaos to revolt on plantations across the South. Maya's plantation is having one as we speak. A few hue men camouflage themselves and bombard the mansion.

The slave owner, his hue traitor, and his family meet butchery and carnage. "C'mon y'all!" yells a hue man. Maya and the runaways follow the man into the muggy marsh. Dark, mushy surfaces make the escape hard. Runaways' feet are sliced by rocks as they swipe at annoying mosquitos. Barking dogs and shouting red slave catchers are on their tails!! Maya runs and runs and runs. JUMP!!! The leading hue man crosses a river, waiting for the others. As Maya debates her thoughts, she is pulled to her subconscious.

Maya sees a tall, shadowy figure running towards her. Behind the shadows, a crocodile-headed hue man speeds to Maya. "Get in the trees and stay away from the water!!" orders the crocodile man. His voice fades as Maya returns to reality. "Get in the trees!" shouts Maya to the runaways. Minutes later, the red slave catchers and their dogs enter the waters to cross. Suddenly, four enormous reptiles rise from under the water. CHOMMPP!! Flesh is shredded from bone while dogs are swallowed whole. " GO!" says a crocodile.

Maya and the runaways exit the trees and move on. "Where we going?" asks wondering Maya. "West Georgia," says the lead hue man. Robert knows some trustworthy hue people near the Georgia/Alabama borderline. Sirius A and B guide the runaways for nights and nights. Near their destiny, one task needed to be conquered for freedom.

Confederate troops had campsites all up the Chattahoochee River, causing an obstacle. Robert thought long and hard about a strategy. Maya found a small military boat hidden behind some bushes down shore. "Y'all two come with me. Maya, you stay here with the others," instructs Robert. Robert and a few hue men tip toe around the sleeping, rebel force. He notices an open box of explosives behind a tree. Robert passes grenades and dynamite to the men. "When I flash the signal, light and throw like hell!" whispers Robert.

Patiently, Robert and the men position themselves. BBBOOOMMMM!!!! Gunpowder barrels detonate, thunderously blowing red men into pieces. Robert and the men swiftly move as they bomb the Confederates. Maya quickly helps the runaways on the boat, losing no time. Robert and the men swim to the moving boat, finally reaching Maya's hand. Robert raises the Confederate flag, disguising the ship from incoming red rebels. America's Civil War dismantles the South's entire living structure. All lines of transportation and communication are severed by Sherman's march to the sea. Confederate leaders are left with no choice but to fly the white flag.

The Civil War finally ends after four years of battle. Thousands are wounded or killed. American nationalism wins. Southern economics would remain poor for decades, as western and northern red men enter the gold mines. To demolish southern pride, Republican officials pass the 13th, 14th, and 15th amendments. Maya and Robert start a new life together, representing hue nationalism proudly. They grow older and raise four children. We are now in post-slavery; let's take a peek at the red man's next level of hypocrisy.

Akasha's Aftermath

The Civil War completely destructs the southern infrastructure, but torn buildings are the least of red people's initial concerns. Southerners worry that the free labor system was too precious to lose, plus free hue beings strike paranoia in former slave dictators. The 13th amendment gives considerable incentives to hues to exercise their alleged "freedom", making Reconstruction the current topic. State governments are in anarchy, providing smokescreens for poor reds and freed hues to pillage the towns for assets.

After Lincoln's assassination, Andrew Johnson assumes the presidency, oddly, bringing Democratic factions to the table for Reconstruction conversation. Methodically, to keep hues down, Johnson knows Democratic powers must forerun the project, turning the plan into a *presidential not congressional* function. A convention of red politicians gather to settle state debts incurred from war, annul ordinances of succession, and reluctantly, abolish all slavery.

Johnson also demanded the 13th amendment be ratified, here are a few exceptions: hues are not allowed to serve on juries or to testify against reds in court, hues are not allowed to marry reds, and still no voting. As time progressed, Republican congress catches on to Johnson's scheme. Confederate war heroes had too much influence in politics, leading congress to believe the south would re-enslave hues if allowed.

Johnson's role in Reconstruction is reduced, clearing the way for radical Republican action. State governments boldly disregard federal laws, still refusing to give hues typical civil rights. The 14th amendment is passed to grant citizenship and equal protection to all hues. This legislation causes race riots throughout the south, which give the illusion that congressional Republican caucus is not working. Confederate states renouncing the amendments were put into several military districts, using federal generals as "probation officers" for the south.

Georgia and other Confederate states linger in "Reconstruction purgatory", denied state representation in both the Senate and the House. Another hammer is cracked upside the rebellious southern reds, the 15th amendment. The right to vote could not be contingent upon race, color, or any other loopholes set to stop hues. After a decade of hard-headedness, Georgia and other southern states finally get with the program.

The Freemen's Bureau bills provided federal aid for hues regarding education, housing, churches, and "employment contracts" created by private land owners. A new marriage between labor, land, and wages support the obliterated economy of the south, called sharecropping.

Contracts vary from land owners; here are a few stipulation agreements: hues are required to pay rent for living on property; half of wages are withheld until harvest season; no wage only a percentage of crops; maintenance of laborer and family is deducted from wages.

Many consider sharecropping "neo-slavery". Rent charged by land owners usually outweigh paid wages, causing debt to the laborer. Interest penalties accrue on unpaid balances, making it nearly impossible to satisfy obligations. However, hue family structures did improve from sharecropping. Hue families birth a lot of children to help with fieldwork. Slavery's oppressive mandates forced families to separate, never creating true bonds between man and woman.

Federal aid is removed from the south after Republicans conspire secretly with Democrats behind doors. Antebellum Confederates have their slave on lock, with no one to save them. Let's look at the geo-red supremacy movement and how they keep a strong vice on hue beings around the world....

Children of the Baphomet

Now you must understand that global red supremacy is a *genetically based* racism. Meaning, red people have a **predisposed fear** of a "hue" planet. The only objective red men have is to keep hues down by any means necessary. The Ku Klux Klan performs most of these duties for the American colony of the global supreme. We have to dive straight into who these people are and where they come from.

Before we start, all preconceived notions you have of the KKK are probably wrong. Racist, country, white-sheet, horse-riding, cross burning images may be running currently in your mind, which is expected. Understand, the KKK is a *sophisticated, advanced, graduate-level, global red secret society*.

It all originates with a group of latter day hue peoples, known as the "Moors". These hues spread out into Europe after Arab nations invade East Africa. Here are a few fields of academia credited to the Moors: alchemic sciences, astrology, music, and what red Europeans call "occultism". Moorish scientists translate all the esoteric knowledge of ancient hue peoples into majority of modern day dialect. Anyhow, the Moors distribute all the ancient information to red men, making them custodians of the wisdom.

Since Atlantis, hue people were **WELL AWARE** of interfacing with a ferocious critter one day. Being proactive, the Moors teach red men, knowing one day they will rule the entire Earth while hue beings are in a state of "dormancy". Red elitists, not all red men, form secret societies to use the Moorish magic out of sight. Freemasonry acts as a grad school for selected, royal red men. Total global domination would result after red men grow smarter and use the ancient knowledge for their own benefits.

After the Civil War, a new secret society pops up in America, terrorizing hues to hinder their progress. Confederate veteran Albert Pike rose in the Scottish Rite Freemasonry ranks to sole Grand Commander. In Nashville, Tennessee, Pike and other generals assemble to politically campaign order for the global red system. High masonry forms the KKK, placing Pike at Grand Dragon, Chief Judicial Officer. Do not forget, the freemasonry is a **WORLDWIDE** order, meaning Pike even has more judicial authority than the American government itself.

The Klan views its tactics as counterintelligence, accepting members but *preferring* masons. Pike brilliantly writes articles, extensively glorifying the chosen, red Aryans and teaching white supremacy to oblivious, gullible reds. As a result, back-wood, inferiors of the red race handle the "police" work for the Klan by the crimes we know them for doing. This actually is America's true law enforcement. In all, the Klan's purpose was to keep the "master-slave" relationship alive.

Now that we understand red, world supremacy, here are a few other branches of the Klan organization for hue retardation in America: hue churches, hue colleges, Hue Boule secret societies, NAACP, Civil Rights Movement of 1964, Hue college fraternities/sororities. Red strategists mob the hue church, charming hue preachers to join the cause. Hue elitists sell out the race, entering corporate America and living as reds. Hue preachers valiantly break the nozzle by hypnotizing hues to sleep with more parables of Jesus the heist....

Choices

As most hues, Maya and Robert are sharecroppers. The landlord receives rent from the couple to use the land and house, paid in pounds of corn and cotton. Maya and Robert support their family with the little left over. If the harvest were bad, the family could starve by depleting all crops just for rent. Lula, their youngest child, usually helps out in the house with washing and cooking. As a young girl, it doesn't take long for Lula to witness violent mannerisms from reds. In particular, red wives of the slave owner.

Verbal abuse is common, and every now and then, some hair pulling. These scenes of terror emotionally scar Lula, lighting a raging fire inside. One night, Lula wept in quiet. She was tired of seeing her parents work so hard for nothing. She cried herself into a deep sleep, yet able to recognize the following reports…"What the!?" says Lula surprisingly. She finds herself in the form of a black cat. "Where am I?" says Lula in her mind.

A hyena-headed hue man is signaling for Lula's attention. "My queen, I have found the men you summoned for. Follow me to their resurrection," says the hyena god. Not sure what he means, Lula follows him down a hall. In a double mirror, she sees a red man in a KKK uniform. Strapped around his torso is a belt configuration, holding up what looks like an open mask around his head with spikes. "Somebody help!!!" cries the Klansman. His eye is badly bleeding, pulsing with puss.

The hyena god goes to a microphone. "Hello Andrew, I want to give you an offer. So far, what could precariously be called your life, you've dedicated a living to causing pain for others. Klansman would call you a hero or a good man. I call you unworthy of the chance you possess to clean your heart. Now we will see if you can go inward to sacrifice the one thing you use to bring calamity. The machine around your neck is a death helmet. The helmet is on a spring stopwatch, if you do not discover the release key in time, the helmet will crush your head. Picture it like a Venus fly trap. The key is behind your eye. Live or die. Your opportunity," concludes the hyena god.

"Fuck you!!!" screams the Klansman. He tugs the chain and the timer goes off. He has 60 seconds. "SHIIITTT!!" shouts Andrew. He sees a medicine box on the ground, inside is a scalpel. Blood oozes from his eye as he tries to prepare himself for excruciating pain. "AAAHHHH!!" screams Andrew. The scalpel pain is too much and frustrates Andrew. 20 seconds. "I won't hang hues anymore! Just please let me live!!" begs Andrew. Lula looks up at the stoic hyena god's face, he doesn't even blink. 5 seconds.

"NO!" panics Andrew. CLAMP!!!! The iron metal death mask closes on Andrew's skull. Blood falls out the helmet cracks. Cat Lula is wowed by the happening. "Oh yes, there will be blood Lula. Come." says the hyena god. He leads Lula to another window. Lula remembers the restrained, hanging red man. He is "Judge Woodrow" from the county courts. He was notoriously known for Klan membership and imprisoning hues on false charges. "GET ME OUTTA HERE!!!" hollers Judge Woodrow.

The hyena god turns on the microphone. "The very fabric of life is complex, Mr. Woodrow. Although you may wonder where you are, I am here to tell you that location is not pertinent to your current predicament. Being a judge in a society has allowed you to poison the atmosphere of justice with your lying, racist ways. The arm of truth has never played a role in your judicial career. Now, I offer the opportunity to really put your arm to the test. The device your legs are strapped to is a reverse pulley.

The key to release you is hidden in the killer bee nest hovering over your arm. Killer bees are cross-bred hybrids. Africanized and European bees biologically concoct a venomous, insane bee. Africanized bees possess a hostile, natural programming, making them very insidious. Since you cannot "feel" the African entities, you will be forced. You will be prized 60 seconds, since you think they qualify as 60% of person anyway.

Consider this a second for every thought. Live or die Woodrow. Your fate." concludes the hyena god. "Go to hell bastard!!!!" says Woodrow swatting bees. BUZZZZZZZ!!!! "AHHHH!!!!" screams swollen-face Woodrow. 30 seconds. By now, Woodrow has been stung to death. PING!!! RIPP!! Woodrow's legs are outwardly reversed, splitting his body in half. "Many more will experience comparable fatalities.

Stay strong, Lula. A boy will be born in a few generations. I will help him as I have helped you. Value your life, Lula. Although your hue woman conditions are challenging, you can strive past them. Keep balance in your heart," says the fading hyena god's voice. The next morning, Lula awoke feeling refreshed. She was immediately approached by the red lady of the property. "Hi Lula, how ya doing?" asks the red lady. Shocked, Lula mugs her, familiar with her bipolar personality.

"You want some breakfast? I will make you and ya ma some! Is your pa around? Ya wanna go to the carnival later? I'm going to give you and ya ma some land. You want a new dress Lula??" nervously says the red woman. Untwisting her braids, Lula checks the woman. "Why you being so nice??' asks Lula. The red woman looks to her right and left. "Come over here child," says the woman. Lula and the woman walk behind the house, in privacy. "Last night, I had a graphic nightmare Lula! A black cat had taken me hostage to a dark alley. Klansmen bodies were piled like pancakes. The slow acting nerve gas flowing through your veins causes you to be numb towards the poor hues. Save yourself or join my congregation!" says the animated woman.

Lula lowers her head, smirking. "Lula I'm serious! I'm so scared I don't know what to do!" wonders the woman. The rest of the day, Lula and the family rested and were pampered by the red woman. New clothes, shoes, and personal items were given by the woman. She wrote a contract, leaving a few lots of property to Lula. The decades danced, taking us to the future. Maya and Robert happily live their last few Earth years. Lula grows into a fine, beautiful caramel hue woman. We are in the 20th century, nearing the pre-Civil Rights era….

Hazel and the Wands of Horus

Hue sell outs have been thrown a few more crumbs from his master by the early 1900s. Reds made sure they were involved with everything hue, from church to hue organizations. To the traitor, working with the red elite is a prosperous investment he cannot refuse. He is the front-runner in hue politics, boasting on hue progression to lull the hue population to sleep.

Clandestine hues are sent to preach in hue communities, paid to keep the sleeping potion plentiful for hues. Hue preachers use Christianity to get hues to accept second-class privileges from "god" and reds. Hues are brain-scrambled to ignore all sources of information from any hue radical using firm action for hue rights. Hue warriors, such as Marcus Garvey, stand up to the beast, fearing nothing.

To counter, red strategists create hue traitors to degrade the power leaders, making them look as if they are violent. Sadly, hue America goes for it. Hue democrats masquerade at ball parties with red vampires. They kiss red babies, riding the fanciest vehicles of the era. After he dines in the governor's mansion, the hue apologist sneaks in expensive hotels with prostitute red women. And when the night ends, he tiptoes in the house to his resting hue wife. Lula has several children, the youngest a girl named Hazel.

One cool night, young Hazel is in a deep slumber. Through the window, two fairies enter Hazel's bedroom. "Shhhh!!!" says one of the fairies. Wheeewwww!! Purple sparkly dust falls to her eardrum. The fairies fly into Hazel's central nervous system through the spinal cord. Cynthia and Denise hop in a boat, rowing to Hazel's primal brain. The fairies merge in with the pineal gland and vanish. Hazel's guardian angels assist her in the South's wild environment.

Denise often whispers in Hazel's ear to keep her motivated. Cynthia massages her aching muscles after long evenings of work. As Lula grows old, Hazel takes care of her. One Friday, Hazel decides to go to a local hangout spot for hues. Hues were dancing and just having a good time. Hazel walked to the edge of the bar, near the bingo table.

Alone, a man sat at the bar, with multiple empty shot glasses. Hazel looks at the man, seeing his eyes rolling backwards. He was very drunk. Hazel tapped the man several times on the shoulder. "Sir! Sir! You alright?!" asks Hazel. Woozy, the man picks up his head and answers. "Yea, yea, yea, I'm aight," says Warren. He rises out the chair stumbling and Hazel catches him. "Warren, where you live? You need to go home!" says Hazel.

Hazel puts Warren's arm around her shoulder to take him home. The two reach Warren's porch. "Hazel, I don't know how to thank you!" says Warren. "Why you get so drunk? You barely could stand up Warren!" asks Hazel. Warren shakes his head. "I be working hard Hazel. Dealing with pulpwood logging five days a week. I drink on the weekend to ease my mind from all the work. It's hard Hazel," concludes Warren. Hazel placed her hand on his shoulder. " You gotta be easy on ya self, Warren," says Hazel. "I suggest you right, Hazel. I like your style, you a real woman," says Warren. "can I take you out sometime?" asks Warren.

Hazel smiles. "As long as Jack Daniels don't beat me to you!" jokes Hazel. The two laugh and continue socializing….

Separate and Beyond Equal

Segregation and the Jim Crow laws tag team to bring red supremacy into the new era. Actually, to the surprise of many, local customs and law enforcement play larger roles than Jim Crow laws. Reds from previous generations instill racist values in their children, since sympathy for hues was becoming more popular in the 20th century.

In addition, segregated socialism makes it very easy for young reds to accept the madness. America's federal courts even accommodate for the neo-red movement by upholding state segregation laws when hues seek civil rights. Southern reds introduce the literacy tests and grandfather clauses to discourage hues from voting participation.

One particular industry, state prisons, use the law to re-glue the "slave-master" relationship. Hue men are heavily discriminated against, driving prison populations through the roof with false convictions. For example, Georgia leases felony inmates to privatized business for cheap, manual labors. Prison wardens and officials collect big bucks from the conspiracy, instituting some of the first signs of prison, slave labor in the country.

By now, more and more hues become educated, demanding equal rights and the birth of the civil rights movement. Before we learn why the NAACP and Civil Rights Act was complete secret society engagement, let's visit why segregation did hues some good for the 100-year period. "Black Wall Street" is a neighborhood in Greenwood, Tulsa, Oklahoma. Reds did not allow hue customers in business, forcing the hues of Greenwood to establish their own empire.

O.W. Gurley, a hue entrepreneur, purchased "hue only" land in the area. Slowly but definitely, Gurley built businesses and residences to help migrating hues who searched for safe territory.

Eventually, "Black Wall Street" had its own banks, grocery stores, libraries, dry cleaners, and many more different businesses. For the first time, a group of hue millionaires successfully stimulate self-sufficient economics for hues. As they usually do, reds get overzealous with jealousy and plan to destroy the town. A massive race riot started after a red girl accuses a hue man of assault. Hues come to defend their brother to find angry red mobs waiting for his release from jail. Reds toss cocktails in hue businesses and even steal planes owned by hues.

In the end, "Black Wall Street" collapses, but not without forever going down in history as true, hue independence. Segregation allowed hues to depend on each other and build "hue integrity". The absence of red intervention was just what hues needed, obviously with the "Black Wall Street" case.

Afraid of hue dominance, red elitists decide it is better to join the rat hole with the hues rather than leave them alone. "Black Wall Street" also showed reds that hues could get organized and violent, which he knows is his detriment. To counter, secret societies flood hue civil rights groups with undercover reporters, both hue and red….

Free At Last?

Hazel and Warren thrive together to experience a better quality of life. While Hazel stays home with the children, Warren works hard for the check. All Warren focuses on is making sure the family has resources. Dealing with the bulky logs strains his body, breaking him down just to survive. Joe Pete, a red man, owns the logging company, scheduling Warren crazy hours because of his work ethic. On weekends, Warren still drinks hard to ease the agony. Exhausted, Warren usually is quiet around the house.

Hazel tries her best to keep her kids trouble-free, using stern, and motherly-love. A few years pass and Hazel has a girl named "Sharon". Sharon, from the lion season, is born in the midst of civil rights chaos.

Resistant hues continue to end segregation. Non-violent peace parties march on Washington and catch billy clubs to the dome.

The newly developed Ku Klux Klan, or police, spray pressure hoses and release hydrophobic canines to attack hues. Over the long haul, the federal government passes the Civil Rights Act. Remember, the Civil Rights Act was **NOT** legislation just for hues. Young Sharon finally gets to discover education without interruption. However, many hue students are given second-hand materials. Outdated books red students no longer used are passed to the hue schools.

But that did not stop lioness Sharon. She involved herself in multiple school activities, gaining popularity from school administration. As a girl, Sharon often dreamed and wondered about life. *I know it is something more than just this. There has to be another side!* thinks Sharon. Sharon studies and studies. Hues and education have always had a love-hate relationship since slavery. Reds restructure the national system, designing everything from careers to law to keep hues down.

In reality, the Civil Rights Movement doesn't do what it is blown up to be. Racism and prejudices still run the country and hues still are in financial depression as a **group**. Young Sharon beats all odds and slays all obstacles for education advancement. She enrolls in a graduate program located in Iowa. The only problem was she was in Georgia. Tenaciously, Sharon pioneers for her future generation by taking on the grueling trip. She bought a little used Toyota for the long journey.

Unsuspecting, Sharon had a big spiritual road block waiting for her. In her childhood, Sharon had two fairies who watched her at all times for safety purposes. "Carole, something doesn't feel right. Can you sense it?" asked Addie Mae. Carole mentally tapped into the galactic magnetic fields. "Yea, I do. C'mon!" says Carole. POOF!! The two fairies disappear to the astral plane and scope havoc. The vampire star had sent a legion of demons to stop Sharon. "This ain't good! We need the reinforcements!" says Carole.

Addie Mae and Carole unite to form the "scorpion goddess". Meanwhile, Sharon drives unaware of the battle about to take place on her behalf. "YOU WANNA GO TO WAR!!" screams the fierce scorpion goddess. ZING!!! She creates a toxic cloud to paralyze the demons. A cosmic, giant cobra falls out of the cloud. "SSSSSS!!!" hisses the space snake. The cobra coils around the demons, but one slips away. SPLAT!!

The demon spits glob in the Toyota's oil compartment. The car starts to smoke hard. *What is going on??* thinks Sharon. COUGH!! The engine starts hacking, bringing the vehicle to a slow halt. "Damn!!" thinks Sharon. She is only a few hours away from Iowa's city limits. To add stress, Sharon is stuck in the middle of a long highway. Checking under the hood, Sharon immediately starts to think of how she can get help. "I can call Diane! She is close to the college and can come get me!" discovers Sharon.

The scorpion goddess is steamed with anger at her captives. "Who sent you!!??" yells the scorpion goddess. Terror-stricken, the peon stars beg the queen for mercy. "The one with all ego! He has sent us, my great mother!" cries the demon stars. The scorpion goddess's eyes turn into fire. "Eliminate them now!!" orders the goddess. Thick, oozing, slimy venom salivates from the cosmic cobra. "Yessss, mother." hisses the cobra. He swallows the demon stars, sending them to forever nothingness.

On Earth, Diane receives Sharon's call and comes to help. While Sharon sleeps waiting, the wolf star sends a pack of black wolves to protect her. In due time, Diane gets Sharon and her belongings. Sharon starts the semester in the foreign state a week later. She triumphs through homesickness and cold weather. The following year, Sharon completes the master's program, creating a powerful foundation. In the 70s, red secret societies pump heroine in hue neighborhoods for the updated "neo-slavery".

Warren passes in the 80s, returning to his heavenly home. He joins the spiritual military to represent Hazel and the rest of the clan. In the 80s, the American red government floods the hue streets with a new poison, crack cocaine. Back in Georgia, Sharon meets a man named "Chuck". Chuck was from Ohio, coming to Georgia with entrepreneurial ambitions. Together, Chuck and Sharon explore Atlanta's opportunities. A year later, Sharon is pregnant with her first child....Nothing was the same from that point on.

Intermission – Breathe 1st

    Please take this time to pause. Breathe in. Breathe out. Breathe in. Breathe out. Breathe in. Breathe out. Good. Grab some water. Get ready for something new! (Elevator music)…..

The Midnight Mirage Presents…

Section Two:
The New Testimony

The Midnight Mirage Presents…

Ch1 – The Black Dot

Pregnant Sharon keeps healthy by proper nutrition and reading, frequently conversing with Chuck on subjects involving hue history. The two read books and watch videos to fully apprehend the depth of the knowledge, with unborn Chad soaking it all. Chuck gives Sharon "The Mis-Education of the Negro" by Dr. Carter G. Woodson to read for more understanding.

Chuck grew up during the era influenced by the greats such as Malcolm X, Marcus Garvey, and Muhammad Ali. He learned at a young age what being hue was all about. Sharon reads to unborn Chad day and night. "Damn! What kinda call is that?! That's terrible!!" screams Chuck. Chuck and Sharon also watch basketball with unborn Chad. "Jordan, for the jam! Michael Jordan with the right hand dunk!" shouts the announcer.

As the months pass, unborn Chad grows. During Mercury's season, Pregnant Sharon's contractions take off. "Magic finds Worthy, great play by the Lakers! So Magic said he would score, post up, and pass and already he's done all three," says the announcer. Chuck watches Pistons vs Lakers one evening. Sharon is in the hospital, alarming Chuck that Chad's birth could be at any moment. "Just relax Sharon, everything is good," says the nurse. Chuck and Sharon have baby Chad the next day, safe and sound.

Sharon was overjoyed with her first, new child. At the same time, bills try to steal her joy. She decided to get certified for teaching and use her gifts to financially support her future. Baby Chad stays with Hazel while Sharon schools. He's getting bigger. Hazel establishes a strong bond with Chad in the early days. Warren's spirit had never left the home, so he too loved his grandson.

Hazel's town, Louvale, was still heavily hurt from the devilish fangs of slavery and sharecropping. It was the mother base for Chad, and his ancestors/extended family members treat him well. Baby Chad intrinsically inherits his deep roots, learning of his ancestor's journeys in the South. Sharon finishes her programs and is ready to go on with her career. She and Chad stay with her sister, Vick, on the $outh$ide of town until things continue to improve. Eventually, Sharon gets an apartment on the $outh$ide too.

Life is tough for Sharon, dealing with financial hardships to survive. We must remember, Chad is born during the "neo-technology" era of red supremacy. Drugs, economic depression, discrimination, and stealth deception are the current tools of destruction for red supremacy. However, hues had one thing on their side that provided medical healing for the bullshit. **RAP.**

Please do not forget the previous stories you have read thus far. **ALL THE EVENTS SYNCHRONIZE.** Anyway, Sharon has a relentless attitude toward providing for Chad. Addie Mae and Carole assist Sharon spiritually. They often whisper words of wisdom in her ear, reminding her she is the true hue goddess. SQUISH!! Sharon exchanges blows with the invading roaches sent by the vampire star.

Head held high, Sharon moves forward. ZZZZIIINNNGGG!!! The hawk star penetrates the atmosphere at the speed of infinite light years. His ember glitter burns up the giant ten-headed roach hovering over Sharon and Chad. Shortly after, Sharon is pregnant with unborn Chase. Time moves on. Sharon gets a teaching position at a hue, private elementary school.

Chad jumps in education like double dutch. Let's see what he has to say about it… Since I could remember, Ma and Dad always were talking about either being black, money, or all the corrupt things folks do. My school was all black, so I didn't see it like they did. Only thing I cared about was Sega Genesis, WWF, Power Rangers, Toys-R-Us, Chuck E. Cheese, Jordans, and all the other kid stuff of the 90s.

Life got real sweet once Chase was born. Nothing is like having a brother. All we do is live to beat Sonic the Hedgehog and finally reach Shao Khan on Mortal Kombat 2. Lights go off. (Undertaker's Theme Song). "Look at this! OHHHHH!! He just got nailed with the tombstone! The tombstone! It's over for that guy!!" yells the announcer. Wrestling for me and Chase was unbelievable. I was used to Dad watching horror movies and twisted Hollywood cinemas.

They used to scare me, but as I grew, I became weirdly attracted to them. In other words, *I grew immune to fears very young.* The things most kids were afraid of, I didn't fear. My parents never allowed me to feel subservient to anything. They always told Chase and me we were kings. Kids on the playground went running when I came around. I guess the WWF was making me ruff. Lol.

Ma got us a house around the corner from where we stay now. Man it's cool to have a big home! Chase and I have a toy room full of gadgets. Life is nice. We see Chuck every now and then. I'm just happy ma is satisfied. I had a friend named "Rich" from school who, ironically, moved to the same neighborhood. I met a kid named "Venny" who stayed down the street. He brings his wrestlers over and we play basketball on my goal. Chad shoots jump shot. SWOOSH! Grabs rebound. Drinks Gatorade. Rap music is big too. 90s rap is so stylish and mental it is making me look at life different. A Tribe Called Quest, Jay-Z, 2Pac, Biggie, Cash Money, and others constantly jam in the radios.

I recall in 3rd grade having an assignment requiring us to read a story. It was about a grandfather and his grandson fishing. Afterwards, the teacher told us to write about an experience we had with our grandfather. Chad looks around the classroom. Kids are talking about their stories. Chad is quiet. A lighter flicks inside Chad. Pain follows. My granddad ascended years before I was born. I always ask mom and grandma about him although it never helps. I want to actually see him. Why can't I see him? How come he died? Why did he die so fast? What was he doing? Questions ran through my mind.

And what's up with this money stuff? I'm confused! How come we can't just go to the bank and get it? Why are we, the blacks, treated *differently*? Chuck talks about money when Chase and I go over his house. He always is warning us about white people and their "ways". I see white people all the time. They *seem* normal to me. I know that white people had black people in slavery in the past. Slavery is very bad.

Chuck talks about white violence and shows Chase and Chad a picture of a hanging black man. I don't like the way it makes me feel. Why would the white people hang him? Did he steal something? Did he kill somebody? What did he do? It just doesn't seem right to me. To be honest, all of this stuff is confusing. The rap music helps because they talk about the same stuff. I wonder how they know. The years change.

Chad's voice starts to crack. Cosmic coal builds internally in Chad, swimming through his bloodstream like fish. "What the?!?!?" says Chad panicking. "Ssssssssss…" says a low hissing noise in Chad. *What in the world is going on??* thinks Chad in his mind. Anyway, 5th grade was critical to my development as a man. Ma had moved on with her life into the next stage. Chuck has disappeared.

Puberty was giving me problems. I recall a key memory that shaped my view of females forever… "Aye Chad, you going to the dance tonight?" asked Rich. "Yea man you know I'm in that joint,' replies Chad. At the time, I had a "girlfriend" named "Shade". Oh girl was in the fast lane for us to be only 10. She would often walk past my class, signaling for me to come out. Sneaking, Shade and I would go behind the trailers to kiss. For all I knew, we were having sex. Chad and Rich pull up to the after school party. Chad searches for Shade. "What's up Chad! How you doing?" asks Shade. Chad's heart pumps fast. She leans over and kisses Chad.

Shade's magic drifts Chad to a polychromatic, psychedelic, varicolored paradise. All the kids dance to music. Chad is in the cut with Shade. Slow jams play. For all I cared, that moment could have lasted forever. The dance ends. Shade kisses Chad and walks away. The dove star blazes into Earth's outer zone. After the dance, Rich and I rode back to the neighborhood with his mom. I couldn't understand why Shade was on my mind so hard. I had girlfriends before, but none like this. I don't know. Anyway, ma had moved on with her life and was prospering.

I had a new sister, Gab. Damn it's cool to have a sister! The girl Gab really just chills. Gab releases a floral, calm pheromone around

Chad, creating bliss in the atmosphere. Time moves on. More kids move to the neighborhood, which are all a few years older than me. The older kids take me under their wing in the streets. I think they like my aggressive, nonchalant attitude.

On the 1st street, I was cool with Tim, Ju, and Skizzle. Of all of them, Tim was the most unique. He was from the West$ide, which was one of the original areas blacks in the city resided. Tim was the type to roast you, fight you, and then give you the shirt off of his back in the same hour. Skizzle was serious about basketball like I was. His dad had played ball with MJ in school. Shit just because of that we had to hoop. And his dad is funny as hell.

Chad and Skizzle walk up to Tim's house. Tim daps up the two. "Shit bruh I got this new Three 6 Mafia, y'all boyz come in." says Tim. "Triple 6 Mafia Presents Underground Vol. 1: 1991-1994" reads the case. Tim turns on the CD player. Chad plays double dutch with the 808s. " Ridin' in the, Ridin' in the Chevy….Ridin' in the, Ridin' in the Chevy….Ridin' in the, Ridin' in the Chevy….Ridin' in the, Ridin' in the Chevy, " plays the track. Chad falls into his subconscious. "Is it that marijuana that got my mind clickin, could it be Erk and Jerk? That got me straight trippin, Dippin' through the greens you so clean, Paul you so mean, a nigga drunk as hell, liquor flowin' through my bloodstream," raps Juicy J. Celestial oils begin to flood Chad's brain.

Chad's eyes turn into mercury. "Demonic mind, why must I love to take so many lives? Why do I leave them suffering, lying there to die? Why do I send their mother pictures just to watch her cry? Why does the devil use me to commit these evil crimes? " raps Lord Infamous. Sulfuric acid clouds form with laser thunderbolts in Chad's mind. BOOOMMM!! Gigantic tombs begin to rise from under the ground. Low rain drops fall. WHHOOOO!!! Tree branches are breaking. SNAP!! "Chad! " yells Tim and Skizzle. Chad wakes up shaking his head. "Bruh what the hell you doing?! " says Tim. Chad looks confused. "What you mean? I was nodding to the shit. Tim, let me borrow this." says perplexed Chad.

Tim hands Chad the cd. Later on, we left to play basketball. Them boyz was looking at me like I was trippin'. I wonder what they were talking about, for real though…. Anyway, 5th grade was about to end, but not without a dramatic close. One day, Rich told me he got word Shade was cheating. It was hard news and I did not believe Rich would lie. I decide to keep an eye on her. Sure enough, I get my answer. I was walking down the hall, when I saw her with this cat Clay that I knew. He stays by Tim in the hood.

Shade and Clay walk, laughing together. Shade leans over and kisses him. Chad shakes his head. Black, crystalline lava starts to stream down Chad's body. Hours pass. Bells ring for the bus. "Yo Chad, you aight?" asks Chase and Rich. Dark gloomy clouds take over the skies. Chad rumbles with powering anger. He mugs Clay with a sharp stare. The bus arrives to the neighborhood to let kids off. Clay gets off and starts walking home. Chad transforms into ChadZilla. He opens the cloud and drops a wild, Titan Cyclops.

All the children scream and run home. "CLAY!! " roars ChadZilla. Clay's eyes widen and he runs home. ChadZilla orders the Cyclops to attack. "AWWWWW!!! " screams the beast. Chase summons a typhoon to swallow the Cyclops. Clay runs in the house. "Chill out bruh, damn!" yells Rich. Chad struggles to stand up. " What happened?" asks Chad. Chase picks up Chad.

" Nothing man, let's go. Rich, Imma holla at you." says Chase. Shit been real crazy lately. It's like when I get mad, I blank out. I'm not remembering any of the things folks are saying I did. Plus it is absurd. So absurd I won't even repeat it. Year 2000 is coming up. All the television talks about is the world ending and foolery. Smh. Last day of school, I went to holla at Clay about Shade. Plus, I figured I should apologize according to Chase. "It's all good bruh. But you wanna know something?" asks Clay.

Chad nods. "Shade two-timed me too dawg. After P.E., I saw her kissing this guy from my class behind the bleachers. Chad laughs. "Wow! Damn, that's crazy. She did us the same way! You think all girls are like that???" asks Chad. Clay rubs his chin. "Let's hope not. All I know is that shit crazy." says Clay. The two dap up. From that day on, I never trusted any female at face value. Years pass and I enter middle school. I still don't hear from Chuck. *I wonder where he is?* Ma tried to call him, but he didn't answer.

Good thing I have Chase and Gab. In society, nothing has changed between black and white people. I still haven't seen any white people be violent, but I don't know. Shade taught me everybody gotta be analyzed. I have to keep my eyes open. Stay on point… Niggaz here in middle school worse than 5th grade. Stuffing tissue down the toilets.

Classes on hall A beef with classes on hall C. Reputation is big. Kids are getting knocked out daily. Lunch money is stolen. It's a jungle. To me, it is very comical. My face card is good with all the kids so I don't worry. They respect me because I don't act fake. Plus they know I'm not afraid. Then Tim goes to the school. And he's not showing any love. I saw him go in a kid's pocket the other day and take his money. Chase told me he saw Tim punch someone and run on the bus. Lol. It's rough out here in these streets. Especially when your face card is not A1. When I look around, everything seems like a version of "hell". Maybe I'm trippin'…..

The Midnight Mirage Presents…

Ch2 – Misery in Malkuth

Chad turns on "Hail Mary" by 2Pac. "Makaveli in this, Killuminati, All through ya body, the blows like a 12-gauge shotty, Uh, Feel me!! Come with me, hail Mary, nigga run quick, see, what do we have here now? Do you wanna ride or die? La da da da da da…" raps young Chad. In middle school, I saw so much turmoil it was outright ridiculous.

Chad walks through Pointe South halls. Pterodactyls fly over Chad's head. Fireballs fall from the skies. Chad shoots a jump shot in gym class. Clank!! Ball rolls behind the bleachers. Chad retrieves the basketball. He sees two students having sex. Chad shakes his head walking away. This life shit really turnt up now. These folks having sex and can't even count to 100 correct. Niggaz smoking cigarettes.

Certain girls have a face card of being known for promiscuous behaviors. I was starting to think my experience with Shade was to make me wake up. Who knows, I could have gotten caught up like this pregnant girl in my class. Basketball got me fully incorporated. It's like a mini-world I can escape to and leave the hoopla. Shoots a jump shot. Clank!! Grabs rebound. Drinks Gatorade. I'm also starting to see betrayal in a more sadistic way. Seeing ma melee through single parenthood battles is fostering merciless emotions in my body. I can't take this shit anymore!!

Chad turns on "Mystic Stylez" by Three 6 Mafia. Chad slips into his subconscious. "What the hell!! "panics Chad. A fiery tyrannosaurus rex stomps toward Chad. ROAR!! The raged rex starts running!! Chad sprints away. A hand places a three-headed, monstrous Cerberus on the ground. ROOF ROOF ROOF!!! "Join the dark side, young Chad."

says a deep voice from above. "Leave me alone!!!!" yells running Chad. A black, smoky cloud with red eyes blocks Chad's route.

Chad falls on the ground. ROOF ROOF ROOF!! Cerberus is closing in on Chad!! The T-rex is behind him!! A raven flies out the cloud. "Come home, my brother." says the raven. "Get away!!!!" screams Chad. Minutes later, Chad wakes up in a cold sweat. By 7th grade, all emotions of me giving a damn have left. Most of my classmates do not understand me. Teachers whisper to each other when I walk in the room. Chad passes a student in the hallway. The student looks at Chad's face. Chad's eyes turn into galactic thunder.

The boy runs away from his open locker. "Bruh, you left your math book!!" yells Chad. I'm starting to think either I'm thrown off or the world is. Chad shrugs his shoulders. Although Chuck isn't around, I could never say I didn't have positive black men in the area. Across the street from Rich, a man named "Mr. E" resides. He may be in his early 40s. Mr. E always preached to the boyz in the hood about education and staying out of trouble. For pocket money, Mr. E would let us cut his grass or help clean up around his place. He also would have contests for us to write on a topic for cash prizes. Topics like "what do you want to do after school? " type stuff.

Most of my older homeboys used to just laugh at Mr. E. Chase and I used to actually do them. Mr. E. always pulls me to the side and talks my head off. I never knew why, but I never ignored him. I always listened. Every now and then, Mr. E. would come play ball with us. Lol. We love hitting him with a crossover to watch him break down. He usually just laughs and says "Y'all young cats supposed to be able to do that!" When I got older, I was thankful to have a real person like him around.

Next door, my homeboy Loc has an older brother named "AB". AB was the "OG" or the original gangster of the hood. I only knew him for being goofy and playing all the time. Loc used to tell me about AB's warrior side in the streets. It was so hard for me to believe because I didn't see that in him. Whenever I saw him, AB talked to me about school a lot. He knew I was really a nerd and admired that. It was confusing because most other kids hated being smart.

"Bruh, stay yo ass away from that wild shit. Just go play ball and keep up ya school work." says AB's echoing voice. Like Mr. E, AB's wisdom was a little confusing for my young mind. He had never lied so I listened to him. Chase has a friend down the street named "Rice". We call him "Alien" in the hood. Lol. Rice's dad, Mr. Martin, was the other black man in the hood who kept me right. You can always find him riding around listening to 2Pac. It may be 20 of us just chilling on the "green box".

For some reason, he would frequently call me to his car to talk. "Stay in the books man. Listen to ya mom. Keep on hoopin'. You can go on to college. Trust me!!" echoes Mr. Martin's voice. Chad nods his head. For fun, me and the boyz go to other neighborhoods and have basketball tournaments. "Paliade", my neighborhood's name, was getting very known from my generation's involvement in the area. I get cool with folks from various hoods, which gained more stars for my face card. In current history, 2001 had some unprecedented events, for me at least.

In Literature class one day, teachers and administrators chatter and chatter about something that happened in New York. Chad sits down to watch the television. " The World Trade Center has been attacked by bombers!! Repeat, the Twin Towers of New York City has been blown up by suicide planes!!!" reads CNN reporters. *What??!! How da hell do terrorists steal an American plane with passengers and destroy a building???* thinks Chad. It just didn't seem right. Why would the terrorists charge America?

A lot of the things Chuck used to talk about start playing in Chad's mind. "I'm telling you! This whole country is corrupt! These white folks trying to kill everybody!!" says Chuck's fading voice. The black history facts I had learned since birth are connecting. A few weeks later, the final piece was added to show me what white folks **really** are like behind the curtains…

One day, Tim and I were walking to his house to hear a new Pastor Troy cd. As we talked, we noticed a tan truck with a Confederate flag approaching us. We were out of his way, but the guy chose to ride close to us. "You niggers need to get out the got damn way!! " yells the white man driving off. Mind you, the year is *2001*. "Fuck You!"

screams Chad and Tim. This was the first, real racist phenomena I had ever experienced in actual time. Chad's internal weather systems get out of line. Low thunder rumbles.

Chad's genetic memory bank opens up. "You dirty nigger!!!" yells the voice of a Klansman in Chad's mind. Visuals of whipped slaves plague Chad's conscious. Anger volcanoes erupt from the pit of Chad's soul. Chad goes home and plays "Crazyndalazdayz" by Three 6 Mafia. Chad falls into his subconscious. Steam rises from the swamp floor. Trees start to madly chant spooky sounds. Chad summons a headless, psychopathic chainsaw man from underground. A half spider/half man creature follows him. 'ZZZZZZZ" cranks the chainsaw man.

"I stand by myself, when it comes to handlin' business, them thangs on the shelf, and that drank to keep me spinnin', and what a nigga start, best believe the Juice gone finish, I feel like Geoffrey Dahmer, chopping bodies in the kitchen," raps Juicy J. "AWWWW," roars a beast. A zombie Nemesis busts through the soil. The dove star flies to the scene, bringing light. She sucks up Chad's creations into a vortex.

Chad wakes up crying and mad. Gab walks in to hug her brother and wipe his tears. Pleasant winds cool Chad's flaming power. The skies turn blue and clear. Thunderbolts cease. I was beginning to criticize and question my nature. Who am I really? Why am I black? When I look at my skin, the dark bronze complexion stares back. But who is the author of the bronze skin complexion of all blacks? Is it Jesus? Chad prays to Jesus.

The vampire star answers, sending more misunderstanding to Chad. "YES!! FEED ME!!!" says the vampire star. A cosmic leech comes and bites Chad. "Ouch!! Damn that hurts!!" says Chad to himself. It seems like every time I ask Jesus to help me shit keeps getting worse. Is Jesus mad? How da hell he mad at me??!! I don't even know that bastard! He probably doesn't like me because I'm black. Fuck him.

I still can't figure all this out, but I'm sticking to what I know. I know I'm black. Let me get into that a little more. Jesus got to go. Weren't the slaves praying to Jesus? How could he let them continue to be in slavery? I thought he helped people?! Maybe black people should leave him alone too. He might be the god of white people. But

I don't know. The rap videos are changing up. In the 90s, niggaz was wearing Africa pendants and throwing up the fist. Now, the rappers' videos are like pornos! I mean damn! It's all money bragging and ass shaking. Black imagery is looking pretty bad.

My own dad not even holding it down like he supposed to. None of my boyz' dads are around. Why the black men leaving the women? Why the black men so damn weak? Why the black women turning to white men? Why are these black women defending these homosexual practices? Why all the black heroes with white women? Why would a woman sell herself for sex??? Smh. Man…..this shit something else. *I gotta represent being black on my own.* I'm going to keep these real lyrics and move on.

Chad laces up his Air Jordan IXs and goes to the court. Shoots jump shot. SWISH! Grabs rebound. Shoots jump shot. SWISH! Grabs rebound. Chad goes for a dunk. SLAM!!! Drinks Gatorade. 8th grade year was one of the best times of life. Chuck shows up every now and then. He's never consistent though.

I decide to try-out for the basketball team and stay focused in school. Money Mitch and Tez, friends from the neighborhood, help me with my skills. My perimeter game needs major work and they help me train. Yank, another cat from the hood, was much older than all of us. He was one of the hardest on me in the younger days. "0 for 50! 0 for 50! Nigga you can't shoot! Where the hell you shooting?? I'm on ya ass!" yells Yank.

Chad goes for a crossover. RIP!! Yank steals the ball and goes in for a dunk. "You gotta do better than that! Pick ya head up! Ya dribble is weak son!" says Yank. Yank forced me to tighten up my game if I was gonna play on the block. I needed the basketball tests if I was to try out for the squad. A few weeks pass and try outs come. Chase is a quick guard so I play him one on one to get my speed up. Chase winds up a dribble. Chad reaches for the steal. "Shit!" says slipping Chad. Chase crosses and goes in for the lay-up.

All I was concerned with was making the team. Chase and I stay up late reviewing basketball tapes and strategies. One player in particular had an effect comparable to no other. "Iverson with the crossover, the fake, the drive, Ohhh!!! Whoa!! Allen Iverson with the unstoppable drive!!" yells the announcer. Chad and Chase are going ham. "The Sixers, Iverson, bothered by Lue, Iverson with the step back! He steps over Tyrone Lue!!" yells Marv Albert.

Allen Iverson was a basketball hero for most kids around my age at this time. One reason was sports. The primary reason was the way he carried himself. "You know I don't wanna be Michael Jordan, I don't wanna be Magic, I don't wanna be Bird or Isiah, I don't wanna be any of those guys. When my career is over I'm gonna look in the mirror and say I did it my way." says Iverson to a reporter. The media and white America bashed Allen Iverson all the time about his "image" such as tattoos, cornrows, and the way he dressed before games.

Society wouldn't just accept him for who he was and I could relate. I felt like Iverson indirectly was representing all the young black boys and men by staying true to himself. It was almost like Iverson was saying all the things I wanted to. Above all the criticism, Iverson was undeniable on the court. Every night someone was doing the Holy Ghost trying to guard AI. *He let his game do all the talking.* His reign perfectly matched my life at the time.

Try-outs were a success. I made the team, finally reaching my goal. The season felt so much like the NBA to me. All I knew was school and practice. I was living the life of an all-star. To me at least. I'll never forget coming through the team banner for home games. The cheering fans created a "March Madness"-type arena. Coach McCoy helped me be a leader and believe in myself. My value system increased with learning to lean on my teammates. Trust was a big issue for me, but Pointe South basketball placed gauzes on my wounds. As the year progressed, I got better and better. My teammate, Darrell, was like the Iverson of the team. Only god knows how many times he made fools out of our opponents.

For the playoffs, we lost from underestimating a team we had beat during the season. That too was a power lesson. 8th grade turned out to be instrumental for my self-confidence. I had come a long way thus far in that department. Now, it was on to high school in a few months. If only I knew what was waiting for me in the bushes....

Ch3 – Kali's Crossroads

"Cuzzzzoo, that boi in high school on these folks!" says Slimm. Daps Chad up. My cousin Slimm was a few years older and already aware of the high school lifestyle. "Them niggaz over there lame, you gotta watch them. The teacher behind me known for snitchin'. Shawty right there by the lockers is the rip. This nigga DC ass goofy!" jokes Slimm. DC walks up. "This is my cousin Chad, he's new,'" says Slimm. Chad and DC dap up. "Ok, Ok, hell yea! Everything gonna be good Chad. Shit straight," says DC. Slimm and DC introduce me to all the old heads of the school.

    All of them stay roasting and joking. Lol. I roast they ass back. It was a big family and the love **felt** real. Don't get me wrong, people were getting slapped or stomped out on the daily. I just stay in my own lane and away from the bullshit. "So DC, what you think about this school shit? You know most folks don't give a damn about it. How do you look at it?" asks Chad. "C'mon man, you know I'm on the school tip. Most people don't realize that the school is just something to help you move on. I only got about a year and a half left. You gotta graduate. Anything else is wasting ya time. Fa real, fa real," says DC.

    Chad nods. "As far as the streets, same shit. I got my lil strap and stuff, but I'm not on that shit. It's just protection. If anything, imma always hook. That street shit don't have any love," informs DC. DC was another older dude who took school serious. Most kids just think they will end up locked up or never graduate. I had been around kids like that since elementary. It was weird because my ma and dad always told me I would go to college. Chase and I been hearing college since forever. I remember when I didn't even know what college was. *I just knew that I was going*. Every day Ma told Chase and me that we were geniuses. We believed her. DC seemed the same way. He was talking about college, trade schools, and other forms of further education. Plus he had all the older girls. I had to slide in on that too.

By now, Tim and the other homies were involved with recording rap tracks. Since we were 8, Tim was always trying to mix or master some type of music. "New York niggaz….they wear they hat forward!" fades young Chad and Tim's voices. We even used the trash dumpster for the beat and recorded with Fisher Price toys. Lol. Those were the days. Older Tim decided to trade the toys for the real deal. My other friend, CR, stamped the movement as "AMP". To me, it was just the same kids I had grown up with. I didn't rap but I was down. As the semester rolled, I bared witness to plenty of fights. Classroom, lunch, hallway doesn't matter. Even heard one of the janitors is a homosexual who preys on students. SMH. This shit hell.

To focus, I keep my head in a book and my eyes on the rim. 9th grade tryouts are in a couple months. It's on. Months pass. Try-outs go good but the program is ass. Well, at least the head coach is. Coach Ham, the varsity coach, seems like one of those sucker characters. Especially towards me. Bruh does shit like kick us out of the gym during practice and makes us do drills in the hallways! What the fuck?! And all the coaches let him! Nobody says shit!! Our season is going bad because the team isn't clicking. 0-some odd number.

The one game we won I took my jersey off after the game and bucked on the other team. I got cussed out bad for that one. Coach Ham couldn't feel my pain as a true hooper. No true hooper likes to lose. So when we won, I was overjoyed with passion. You would think a coach knows that. Smh. I remember when it was time for some 9th graders to move to JV.

People were getting picked and it was down to me and my boy Cayo. Chad looks at Cayo. Cayo looks at Chad. Cayo and Chad burst out laughing. Cayo and I had been cool as hell for a minute. He played in the low post with me, so I had to get cool with him. I didn't care if they picked me or Cayo. He's still my dog… I got picked, but Coach Ham still was stiff on me.

Ch3 – Kali's Crossroads

After the season ended, stuff started changing, for the worse. Some of the older dudes in the school started to get jealous because we didn't let them in our movement. It wasn't animosity, they just didn't understand we were all *home-grown, neighborhood kids*. It wasn't a gang or anything. Just stuff we had done since I was 7. Tensions thicken the air, segregating our side from another group of niggaz. Next thing I know, a person cool with one of my friends gets jumped. 50 pennies, as I call him, is cool with my friend Rock for some bewildering reason. He's one of those "internet pranksters". "Yea man, yea man this AMP! AMP on yall niggaz! Fuck yall! What yall wanna do??'" cries 50 pennies.

There had been several occasions where he had started something we had to clean up. Only this time, he got himself involved with the wrong folks. It was some dudes we were cool with for a long time. Accept now, 50 pennies has muddied the water. It's causing people to gravitate more to the side they originated with. I often went to talk with the heads of the other gang to neutralize the situation. "C'mon now, y'all know damn well this shit ain't serious, man." says Chad. "Man, I'm saying though what the hell wrong with this nigga 50 pennies?? Bruh got us fucked up talking reckless," says Rue.

Chad shakes his head. Slimm was real cool with Rue when I first met him months ago. I had been in his house and everything. The rest of Rue's side were other dudes who had A1 face cards on the $outh$ide. So this situation with 50 pennies was not so easy to get out of. As time went on, Rue's side kept bucking so we bucked back. He wouldn't listen, so war was declared. At first, it started off with fighting. To me, fighting and wrestling was fun so I didn't mind it. They were usually group brawls. Most of these dues are way older than me. I was getting stronger and stronger. Crazier and crazier. 9th grade ends, which was fine with me. That hostile school environment was getting old. Oh, how wrong I was. Doorbell rings. "Bruh what the hell happened to you??" asks Chad.

Tim was standing with blood on his shirt. "Shit, just got to hooking with this nigga. Bruh bit my ass on the lip." says Tim. Chad grimaces. I was so busy hooping, a lot of the time I wasn't around most of the nonsense. Slimm would tell me stories and I would cry laughing. The next year, I'm back at it for try-outs. NBA is getting closer. Chad laces up Jordan IIIs. "Aye bruh, pick me up!'" yells Chad. Game starts. Chad dribbles up. In and out on two defenders. Gathers step. Up and under lay-up. "Mmmmm," says the bench. "Get back! Get back! Get back!" ordered Chad. Chad intrudes the passing lane for the steal. Dunk!!! "Ohhhhhhhh!!!" explodes the gym.

Coach Ham mugs Chad with a sour look. Chad remains humble. Days pass and try-outs end. I couldn't even sleep. All I could think about was the team list. Sunday comes and Chad rushes to the school. Chad searches for his name. Looks up and down. Looks down and up. Looks right to left. Looks left to right. Chad blinks. Chad looks again. I was paralyzed when I saw my name absent from the list. *My performance was good. What went wrong?* thinks Chad.

Thoughts of Coach Ham and his hatred ignite rage inside. Chad laces his Jordan IIIs. Shoots jump shot. Brick!! Grabs rebound. Shoot fade-away. AIR BALL!! Grabs rebound. Shoots jumper. CLANK!! Burgundy mists start to cloud Chad's mind. Chad holds his head. Chad runs home. Grabs CD player. Plays "Electric Relaxation" by A Tribe Called Quest. The clouds disappear. My life was turning down a road I was unfamiliar with. Basketball was my escapism from the shit I didn't want to deal with.

Racism, economic hardship, gang beef, and a boat load of other stuff were weighing my head down. I was tired of waking up to it. It was like a bad tattoo. School basketball is a thing of the past now. Guess I gotta find another Lasik surgeon. All I do know is one thing. **I DON'T GIVE A DAMN ANYMORE**. The only good times are with Ma, Gab, and Chase. More basketball and music medicate when they aren't around. Especially Gab. It's something funny about her. Somehow, she can suppress my colossal energy. Like a floating dove or something. Lol. I'm tripping.

In school, the gang wars continue as usual. Every day it's mugging and gossiping. It's even females working for these niggaz. "Aye, I gotta check myself in the mirror real quick. My undershirt crooked," says Chad. "Yea I need to use the bathroom," says Skizzle. "Mhmm cause ya got crumbs all over ya face my guy!" jokes Slimm. Chad laughs.

Ch3 – Kali's Crossroads

While I fix my shirt, Slimm starts telling us about T-Mac balling last night. Bathroom door slams open.

A group of boys with black flags walk to the back of the restroom. We ignore them until we are interrupted by noise. "Why the hell you run! Scared ass boi! Killa, beat this duck, " orders the GD leader. I peep around to see the GDs surrounding a curled up boy. "I didn't know man! Man I swear I didn't see y'all!! Please don't hit me, PLEASE!!!" whines the boy. GDs start mobbing the poor baby. Smh. *Just another victim*, thinks Chad. "Let's dip, these folk trippin'," says Slimm.

We all leave and head to our classes. The day goes on as usual. A few days later, I was in Coach Ham's world geography class. He was a horrible teacher, so I just napped to dream about basketball. All respect for Coach Ham was as valuable as used tampons to me at this point. Plus my work was always done, so it's cool. I could never overstand Coach Ham's real issue with me. Was it my friends? Was it me? Chad shrugs.

Someone knocks at the door. "I need Chad. And grab your stuff. "says the principal. Coach Ham mugs Chad with a slick smirk. Chad mugs back. I was always harassed by administrators so I figured this was the usual chastisement. Walks past principal's office. Chad's face turns confused. Principal opens bus lane door. Chad sees a line of police cars. "What is this??" asks Chad concerned. I see Slimm and Skizzle handcuffed. "We have you on camera after a student reported an assault. You are under arrest," says the principal.

Officer slaps cuffs on Chad. Chad starts hallucinating. Visions of chained slaves play in Chad's mind. Chad sees Maya and Sengbe being thrown on a boat. "Hell Naw!! Man hell naw!!" panics Chad. A white cop walks up to restrain Chad. The cop's uniform transforms to a KKK robe. "Nigger we gone hang you boi!!!!" says the fading Klansman voice. Chad is put in the back of the car. Cop is driving to the station. Chad slides around the back. Chad sweats hard. Illusions of a mob of yelling white people cloud Chad's conscious. "Hang that nigger!!!!" yells a woman in the crowd. I was a minor, so I was taken to juvenile.

Slimm was taken to county. Skizzle was a year under county limit. Chad is led to a holding cell. The bright lights are blinding Chad. Door slams!! Psychopathic imagery cycle Chad's mental. Cold temperatures turn Chad into a skeleton. Worms and beetles crawl out of Chad's eye sockets. Hours later, my dad came to get me out. We return to the school so I can enlighten the administrators. "And then they walked to the back of the bathroom. I heard them chumping the boy off for not fighting. Next thing I know, Air Force Ones are seen whopping him upside his head," says Chad.

The principals did not believe me and kept giving me a hard time. Chad heads home. Court dates raid my mailbox for appearances. Each time I go, it's the same shit. My anger levels have topped. All this explaining myself shit is old man. Why the fuck all this shit keep happening to me?? The temperature's rising in the streets. You can't even hang out in the hood without always being on alert. I can't walk Gab like I used to. Open mailbox, summons. A few weeks pass by. Open mailbox, summons. More weeks past, summons. Two months later, the court carousel is finally over.

When it came down, the damn boy didn't even know who I was. All that shit was for nothing. I told them fools that months ago. Doorbell rings. "What's up bruh," says Chad. Daps DC up. "You coming to Rock's house?" asks DC. DC spots some biscuits on the stove. "Yes sir, let me get them guys!" says DC playing. Chad laughs. "Yea you got it. Preciate the jeans too," says Chad. Chad hands DC some jeans. "Fa sho, anytime man. Anytime." says DC.

In the streets, AMP was involved in fights and beefs damn near every day. Everybody is hoping in the whip. Chad is walking up. "These niggaz ain't fighting no more, Chad. Just stay out this shit man," says Slimm. When it would be a fight, I dove in to transform into a monster. All the personal pain was unleashed on people in the streets. I was in the trenches daily. I got lost in the chaos… "Bia, Bia!! Why you actin' like a, like a, Bia Bia!! Why you fussin' like a, like a, Bia Bia!! Why you lookin' like a, like a, Bia Bia!! Why you frontin' like a, like a, Bia Bia!!" raps Lil Jon and the Eastside Boyz. People push each other on the dance floor. "Well pour out the Henn and Coke and fire up that dro. It's Ludacris from Old National and Godby Road, the block is sold, clear, then I shock the globe." raps Ludacris. Niggaz run around the club like wild animals. Fists swing left and right. "Ohhhhhh!!!" goes the crowd.

Ch3 – Kali's Crossroads

A dude just got slammed on the pool table. "M-A-F-I-A!!! M-A-F-I-A!!! M-A-F-I-A!!! M-A-F-I-A!!!" a mob screamed. "37 HARD HEAD!! 37 HARD HEAD!! 37 HARD HEAD!! 37 HARD HEAD!! " shouts another crew. The gangs collide like rugby players. "Security! Security! We need security on the floor! Security!!! " cries the DJ. Every weekend, scenes are like this all over the $outh$ide.

Gang violence is taking over. Old folks scared. It's just out of hand. My mind is spinning from the nightmare merry-go-round. This shit is repetitive. Who can I trust? Teachers? Administrators? Coaches? Chad shakes his head. Temperatures rising. Chad throws water on his face. Months travel by. Daps DC up. "I'm about to be done with this shit bruh! Only got a few more credits! I'm outta here soon man!" cheers DC. Chad turns up. "Hell yea bruh! You did it man! Many don't make it out this cage. Damn, I'm happy for you dawg!" says Chad.

DC started coming to school for half days since he was almost complete. "Aight bruh, Imma see you later on. I'm gone," says DC. Chad and DC part ways. Smh. That was the last time I ever was gonna see DC… The next morning, skies were gloomy and grey. Creepiness danced in the thick fog while I walked to the bus stop. I couldn't tell what it was, *but something wasn't right*. I went to school and the day seemed usual. Loc and I ate lunch like we always did. "Yea bruh you gotta hear Tim new beat. Shit hard, trust me," says Loc's fading voice.

When lunch ended, Loc and I separated for 5th period. I headed to the bathroom before the bell rung. I got 8 minutes. Chad exits the bathroom. He sees a crowd of people circling a fight. It is Loc and a rival gang member. Chad is snatched into his subconscious. Black clouds begin to stretch across Chad's inner mind. A church choir begins to chant. The Phantom of the Opera starts playing eerie tunes on the organ.

Mercury rain drops fall from the skies. Chad morphs into Baron Samedi. Voodoo zombies rise from under the ground. Students scatter. Chad Samedi conjures a 20ft werewolf from a tomb. "Owwwwwww!!!" howls the werewolf. Loc's eyes get big and he runs. The organ is getting louder. The choir is raising tempo. One of the football coaches tackles Chad. "Chad!! Chad!! You alright!!!" screams the coach. Chad returns to reality. "Yea, yea I'm good!" says startled Chad.

My heart is beating fast as track runners. Blood is all over my shoes. My shirt is torn. Janitors are mopping up a pool of blood. They are putting brown, powdery sand on it. Students are out of control. The school is a zoo. Chad is thrown in an empty room. *What happened now!?!?* thinks Chad. In walks the principal. "Chad, what have you done!!" cries the principal. Behind him, the bleeding boy is accompanied by his mom. She's fussing and shouting. I examine him holding his ruby red face.

"Did I do that?!?!" Chad asks himself. More and more administrators come in to criticize me. All the blabbering is drowned out my ears by my deep thoughts. *All I remember is a black screen. Man I'm not getting this shit!* thinks Chad. My body starts irrationally itching. "What the hell now! " ponders Chad. Chad blanks out while teachers complain. It was Friday and Ma put me on lockdown. She took all my rap CDs. I guess she thought it was doing something negative to me. She was wrong. There was something else causing my inexplicable actions. The music was actually soothing my "Hulk" mode.

Chase and I dialogue about everything that had been happening. He was the only person who knew me well enough to help me out. All Saturday, I did some major soul searching. *If I can pinpoint my problem, I can heal myself,* thinks Chad. Sunday morning, the fam and I eat breakfast as always. Phone rings. "Hello?" says Chad. "Bruh…DC dead." says Slimm in a low voice. His statement was so mind-altering I was lost for words. "Man stop playing." says Chad nervous.

Slimm proceeded to tell me DC had called him Saturday. He explained how he was walking to the gas station with a civilian friend of his. The guy was never involved in fighting or anything related. A group of rival gang members rode up on him talking trash. "Leave him alone! He ain't got shit to do with this!!" says DC's echoing voice. DC and his friend got jumped by the rival gang. Slimm said he was eating crab legs and DC pulls up pissed. The way he described DC's anger was unheard of to me. I had seen DC mad, but never like this. 50 pennies drove DC to a party where the rivals were chilling.

Slimm says DC unloads at the gang. Simultaneously, AK-47s fire off at DC. We hung up and time slowed down. Tears fall from Chad's eyes. The same night, another young girl was killed on the other side of town. For the following weeks, I entered a silent state of being. Most of the time, I play past times of Chuck E. Cheese in my mind. Where have I come? How did I get here? Why is my life shifting so much?"

Local gang wars lead to the death of two teenagers in shootings over the weekend. Brutal gang fight on Friday afternoon instigates retaliation," reads news reporter. The media was using the fight to justify the deaths, which created guilt inside. My character was being shot at by the world. Sometimes, I thought death may be better than dealing with this shit. My support system motivates me to stay strong. My older sister, Laurie, keeps me focused with words of encouragement. All the neighborhood older men fill me with confidence and hope. Ma and Gab show me real love.

Slowly, my heart recovers from the blows I was taking. I get back to hooping and music. I retire from the sickness in the streets. My tribunal session went favorable, beating the expelling hammer they tried to hit me with. First day of school the following semester, I can't even get off the bus good without principals crabbin'. Rich walks up and daps Chad. "You straight bruh, don't even worry about these folks. Fuck em'," says Rich. "You right man. I just wanna do this work and talk to the females. I'm drained out on all the other shit," replies Chad.

Up walks Thomas. "Boy you fat as hell, damn nigga!? 'roasts Rich. Thomas' face turns upside down. "But your breath smell like you ate a vomit burger!! 'roasts Thomas. Chad starts crying laughing. This is usually what Rich and Thomas were doing, all day. Not to forget they both funny as hell. Hey, at least it's not a shootout. Another difference this year is the way people treat me. Boys and girls. It's like they romanticize what I had done in the fight. Like it was *cool*?! That whole thing caused so much hell for me, admiring it was nowhere near my schedule! Plus my patnah died?! Hell naw!! So I de-hype it when folks bring it up. Even more females jockin' this year. Smh. I had made good grades and no one ever pumped that up. Or how I always got my hand up answering questions. Teacher can barely get the question out and Chad already on it. These clowns are stupid.

My credits got fucked up from the fight when I failed two classes. Two of my teachers wouldn't even let me make up the missing work.

It was only a few weeks' worth. "Well you will fail anyway. Chad, you just are not gonna make it. Just give up ok?" says Ms. Medina. My literature teacher was the only one who had my back. Mr. Sermons was that teacher that would call me out although the whole class was talking. "Chad come outside bruh," says Mr. Sermons. *Damn again!?* thinks Chad. "Nigga what the fuck are you doing?! You got to realize you bigger than the small playing you doing. You smarter than all these kids!! I know about that fight you got in last year. That ain't you. You know damn well it ain't. I been knowing you since you was 14. Boy you can't fool me! Get ya shit together man. What's ya mom's number? You know you not tryin' to see her!" says Mr. Sermons.

Chad speed shakes his head "No". He always had my ma's number but he never called her. "Man that shit gonna be OV when I get home! Damn he gonna call this time!?" worries Chad. Ma gets home later that day. Everything is normal. The school year continued. Months pass. The year ends. Ma has decided to go back to get another degree. The only problem is the college is in South Georgia and 3 hours away. We pack up and leave when summer came. All the memories of the $outh$ide play in my mind as we ride down the highway... There are cotton fields everywhere. Confederate flags flying on houses. This shit crazy all ready. Smh. 12th grade went swell from start to finish.

Chase and I just keep to ourselves, working on getting outta high school. This year may have the most hours my iPod has ever played. All the students know me for is the Atlanta boy on the music. I met another dude, Phillip, who was from the A too. His older brother, Bama, had moved down for educational advancement in life. Bama assumed the role as the old head for giving me wisdom. They too were from the $outh$ide and used to the customs of the streets.

Bama was a good example of a brotha who made it out to do bigger things. He was working hard for his goals. Down the line, he ended up getting a recording deal with Young Jeezy and CTE. Months pass. I made it to graduation! Plus an all-time record of high grades for my entire school career. Regardless of all the hataz, I made it. Ma helped me enroll for a summer program to enter college. I always knew I was coming but now I'm actually here. Damn it feels good....

Ch4 – Heart Ascension

Chad turns on a 2Pac DVD. " You can spend minutes, hours, days, weeks, or even months over analyzing a situation; trying to put the pieces together, justifying what could've, would've happened…. or you can leave the pieces on the floor and move the fuck on." says 2pac's echoing voice. "My mama always used to tell me, "If you can't find something to live for, you best find somethin' to die for." says 2Pac during the interview.

"You read a lot?" asks the interviewer. "All the time, I'm really into books," says 2Pac. "What type?" asks the interviewer. 2Pac puts his hand on his chin and lights a blunt. "Mastering the Art of War, Thoughts of a General, How to Win an Argument Every Time, The Buying of a President…uhhh. What's that book I got? The Russian Guy?" 2pac asks his patnah. "Stalin," replies the man. "Stalin, I got that. A lot of different things. But mostly shit on what built generals and what made countries and uh…I wanna read what Clinton reads. Cause he do the same shit I do, but don't get in trouble for it!!" says 2Pac. The interviewer laughs.

"All his homeboys commit suicide, he gets caught with his pants down in the bathroom and this nigga is STILL THE PRESIDENT!?!?! I got women you know marching outside my shows, THIS NIGGA IS STILL THE FUCKIN' PRESIDENT!!! I'm 24, he's 40! What's his excuse!?!?" says 2Pac.

Interview continues. "The Bible was tellin' us they had special people, I got shot 5 times! One! Two! Three! Four! Five! And I got crucified by the media and I walked through with the thorns on! Had shit thrown on me. I'm not saying I'm Jesus but we go through that type of thang every day! We don't part the Red Sea but we walk through the hood without getting shot, you know what I mean?! We don't turn water into wine but we turn muthafuckin' dope fiends and dope heads into profitable, productive citizens in society! We turn words into money! So I believe God blesses us, I believe God blesses those that hustle and those that use their mind and are *overall righteous*! I believe that your karma and everything you do bad comes back to you. So anything that I'm doing that's bad, imma suffer for it! But in my heart I think what I'm doing is right! You know what I mean? So I feel like I'm going to heaven! And I think heaven is just when you sleep, you sleep with a good conscious. You don't have nightmares. Hell is when you sleep and you see all the fucked up things you did in your life. And you just see it over and over again. This is what's real and all that otha shit is to control you," concludes the 2Pac interview.

I would often watch Pac's interviews for encouragement. He was like Iverson, a real brotha who stayed true to himself. And his knowledge is deep. I was glad that I didn't care what society thought about me. That's pretty much all Pac and AI showed me. People always gonna push you, black or white, to conform to their standards. These damn spoiled ass Americans think everything has to be catered to them. Smh. They can kiss my ass 1,000 times. I'm just gonna do my school work and enjoy college... Thomas had moved down to attend the same school. He stays in a campus dorm, which is co-ed.

Chad winks. His roommate, Rob, is cool too. Bruh is from the Ea$tSide of the city and a real hustla. Like myself, he majored in business. The college life is A1 too. It seems like no matter where you go, your original face card follows. All the dudes around here get cool with me from basketball mainly. Some of these older chicks a lil stiff, but it's all g. Damn near a million girls here. And they got a stooopid ass basketball facility here. Weight rooms, treadmills, bikes, rock climbing, fencing, boxing, hooping, and anything else you can think of. Ma, Chase, and Gab are all doing good.

Everyone is acclimated to the new lifestyle. Watching Ma in the books hard keeps me on my shit. Down the street, I got cool with a brotha named Kevin from high school. Kevin had been through a lot and was trying to survive on his own. His parents had a terrible domestic situation, so KP was solo. I always go holla at him to keep him positive. I can't count how much real shit he has told me.

"Thomas, let's go see what KP talkin' about," says Chad. Thomas and I head to KP's spot to kick it for a while. "What's up with y'all boyz? C'mon in," says KP. KP had the new Assassin's Creed on Xbox. Me being a game freak, the modern graphics blew my mind as I watched the gameplay. Henry was also over KP's house. He was a tall white kid from high school, real cool. Hours pass. Henry and KP take shots of liquor. We all just chillin'. Now, it's about 10 p.m. "KP, you got some green?" asks Henry.

KP goes to his room. He come backs with two blunts. I had never smoked on the $outh$ide. The homies did, but I thought it would hurt my basketball skills. So I was like Ronald Reagan. Lol. I was a lil older now and didn't look at it the same way. Plus I had been through so much shit I thought "Fuck It".

We all head to KP's van. Thomas had never smoked either, so he joined. At this point, I was wondering what it was gonna be like. It was confusing because half of the country likes it and half doesn't. Damn following everyone else, imma see for myself. Down here in college, all I see is white people smoking weed. Drinking beers. Obviously they don't give a shit and it's their parents passing the laws. Chad hits the blunt.

"Now I'm High, Part III" by Three 6 Mafia goes off in Chad's mind. Chad's insides start feeling light. Head is bobbing. Shit is getting funny. Lol. My hands are tingling. Lol. "Triple Six, Trip, Triple Six, smoked out, Now I'm high , really high, mane I'm about to shout." goes the hook. Damn, I ain't neva heard my heart beat like this before! Chad is smoking. We get up to exit the van and my legs feel like silly putty.

Thomas starts transforming into a cartoon character. Lol. *This nigga done turned into Porky the Pig!!* thinks Chad. Chad bursts out laughing. Thomas' pig-like face starts laughing in slow motion. "Stop!! Please stop!!" laughs Chad. The laughter is getting out of hand now! Suddenly, my stomach starts doing the "Rumble in the Bronx". KP gave me some pizza to eat. The laughing just won't stop. "Hahahahahahaha!!!" maniacally laughs Chad.

Chad slowly becomes the Joker. "Dance, my jester puppet, dance!!" laughs Chad Joker. He metaphysically attaches puppet strings to Thomas' back. Thomas is forced to dance like a foolish doll. I realized it was late, so I headed home for bed. Still under Mary's potion, Chad falls into a deep slumber... Chad finds himself in a spacecraft cruising through the astral plane. Lights are flickering on and off. It's foggy as hell. *What is that noise?!* thinks Chad.

A heavy, breathing machine-like entity was standing in the shadows down the hall. Black ravens hover over Chad. "The darkness is with you, human Chad. But you are not a god yet," says the deep voice. The footsteps are approaching. "Who da hell is that!!" yells Chad. The machine-man continues to breathe through the respirator. "Your mental toughness has served you well." says the voice. It's getting closer. When the smoke clears, Darth Vader stood in the doorway.

Chad is marveled to see Vader. 'What are you talking about?" asks Chad. "Join the dark side, young human Chad," orders Vader. Chad squares up with Vader. "So you the muthafucka causing me all this pain!?!?" yells Chad. Chad charges Vader. Vader disappears and reappears on the other side of the room. "Damnit!" says Chad. He runs straight into the wall. Vader uses telekinesis to throw Chad across the room. "You cannot defeat me, young human Chad. Join my congregation in the dark clouds. Your mother has sent for you," says Vader. Chad charges Vader again. Vader pulls out a mercury light saber and swings at Chad.

"Control your fears, young physical man. Your destiny lies with me, person of flesh," says Vader. Chad tries to run out the room. Vader magically shuts the door. "What the hell you want with me?! I don't even do shit!! Just leave me alone!!!" shouts Chad. Purple, mercury raindrops start falling. Vader starts rearranging Chad's neck muscles to choke him. "I find your deficiency of faith offensive, young dead man," says Vader.

"Get out my mind!!!" screams gasping Chad. Vader releases Chad. "I will see you soon, human Chad. Do not forget where your true allegiance is," says Vader. Chad wakes up sweating. The semester rolls on. College life is all I dreamed and better. Grades are good. I'm hooping every day. It's too bad a lot of kids never get to experience this. I guess it isn't for everyone. The weed is helping me spiritually in a way I did not expect. It was like I became one with nature and nature trusted me. My cognitive skills have never been this sharp. Everything about life seems *clearer*. You can see through all the bullshit easily. Maybe that's why the government demonizes it. Smh.

Freshman year ends. It was time to declare majors and I was unsure. I was taking an accounting class currently. "Chad, you good at this. I really think you should major in Accounting. It's hard, but when you're done, you will be glad you did it. Trust me!!" says Mrs. Oliff. Mrs. Oliff was my teacher and she always told me stuff like that after class. She had a lot of faith in me for some reason.

Since I was 5, I always wondered about the mysteries of money. Accounting just may be it. I'm going hard in Financial Accounting class. *Assets = Liabilities + Equity. To increase an asset, expense, or loss, debit. To increase a liability, revenue, or gain, credit*, thinks Chad before a test. *Johnny purchases two boxes of inventory on credit*, reads the question. *Debit inventory and credit accounts payable*, thinks Chad. Chooses "C". This accounting shit is too easy! It's like my brain is a mega, hyper technology, fiber optics system.

Maybe it's the ganja. All the things I couldn't figure out in the past have been revealed to me. Racism and that whole thing. Government secrecy. Dumb shit black folks do. It all makes sense now. The semester ends and Ma has completed her program. She has done it again!! Ma had sacrificed and been through battle after battle to make it. I was happy for her. Chase, Ma, and Gab move out. Thomas moves in and we get a few other roommates. Ma got me connected with a white woman named "Michelle". She was the coordinator of a computer lab on campus and gave me a job. Plus Michelle is major cool and genuine. She is a good example for white people to me.

Time moves on and semesters rotate. The accounting classes are getting tougher, but it's all good. The rap game has switched again to a new era of sound. A lot of it I can't get with. Gucci Mane, a rapper from the A, was dropping a new mixtape like every week. I had been listening to Gucci since I lived on the $outh$ide. He had almost lost his life and fought a wicked trial. He prevailed in the end, crushing rap in consequence. I could relate to the court circus, so I grew with his music. They even got this other weed called "loud". Man this shit here...Smh.

My creative genius flows faster than ever. School is fun. Life is sweet. I was entering, the second phase of college, "major classes". These were all my high-level accounting classes. Intermediate Accounting I-III, Income Tax, and Accounting Information Systems to name a few. These were critical semesters and grind time. I had to stay focused. Chase had moved down for college to start his next stage in life. We were all living the typical college life. Bills and broke. Financial struggles were so normal it was ridiculous. Days with no food. You name it, it happened. We were in the survival game where income is outweighed by expenses.

The infamous "rat race". I just use the green to keep my head up. Chad is watching "Paid in Full". Ding dong! Opens door. "What's up dude? Thomas home?" says unknown person. Chad mugs the guy. "Oh I got it bruh," says Thomas. As I walk off, Thomas hands buddy something but I don't know what. It looked real fishy. "Damn bruh you not trappin' are you???" asks Chad. Thomas scratches his head. "Shiiit, oh na I just had some green I gave him," says Thomas nervously. He looks real suspicious the way he answered. It wasn't smooth enough.

Weeks pass. Thomas' behavior has been real sketch lately. I haven't been seeing him go to work. I don't even know if bruh goes to class. I leave in the morning, see him on the couch. I come back that afternoon, he still there. "Damn I had a long day. What's going on," asks Chad. Thomas opens his eyes. "Shit nothing really, I just woke up a few minutes ago," replies Thomas. Chad's clock says 3:25. "You didn't have to work or go to class??" asks Chad.

Thomas scratches his head. "Shiiit, I mean...I don't think we had class today and I don't work the hours I used to," answers Thomas. Chad nods and walks off. Bruh talking real greasy about his priorities. I thought folks came down here for school! Seems to me, some still think we on that same high school shit. Smh. I came down here to achieve greatness. Man I have come so long with this accounting. Those white kids are always giving me all kinda looks when I walk in class.

Chad walks in and sits down in the front row. "How does this nigger come in here answering all these questions! I am appalled by his splendid allegories and swagger! He walks in here with a white t-shirt, camouflage cargo shorts, an African pendant, Jordans, and obnoxiously rapping! All the teachers like him! I have to visit them every day to brown nose! They don't even remember my name! That's not fair! My father is a well-respected mayor in town! How does he outshine me! How does he know all this knowledge! *Smh, I just don't get it!!!* thinks white student next to Chad. I am receiving accounting rewards and meeting partners of big firms.

I got these old white men laughing from jokes about life on the $outh$ide! Who would have ever thought! I'm blessed!!! Man I'm too far to slip! I gotta watch Thomas, this fool trippin'. I got too much to lose…Jewels, Thomas' younger brother, had moved in with us during the summer time. He is in high school and the polar opposite of Thomas. Where Thomas was passive, Jewels was aggressive. Where Jewels was hard, Thomas was soft. Jewels was a kid who jumped off the porch early. I saw a lot of potential in him because he reminded me of myself.

Thomas did not understand the street element imbedded in Jewels. Chase and I did, so we took him in like one of our own. Weeks pass. Jewels and I are growing a real good bond. I put him on game when it came to the ins and outs of life. I saw he took his future for real and I wanted to help him. Hell, we barely see Thomas now. Every now and then, he would run in for 2-3 minutes and run out. Chase, myself, and Jewels keep each other uplifted with countless conversations about the "real".

I show Jewels my basketball techniques and train him. His style is A1, quick and persistent on both ends of the ball. His grades are turning up and all his teachers like him. Bruh really doing his thing. For experience, I sneak him into some of my business classes so he can breathe college. He brags all the time about how this is the apex of his academic career. His soul is also pure.

Most of my time is spent searching for more clues about life. The streets had taken Jewels for a spin too, so he comprehended the importance of spirituality. "Shit bruh, we gotta stay strong. It is hell not having money around this bitch. We gonna be out one day though," says Jewels. "Yea because it's all a test. A lotta niggaz out here selling their soul for a pair of rims. Women out here selling theirs for a Chanel bag.

It gotta be something on the other side for the real people. The ones who don't fold to the pressure. The ones who keep their integrity. Smh. It's not many of them. We gotta just keep our faith in God and we will be good. I know we will," says Chad. 30 minutes go by. I notice Mrs. Rosemary walking up. She is a white woman my mom was cool with here. "How ya doing Chad?" says Rosemary sadly. "We good. What's wrong with you?" asks Chad. "My daughter, she has been having some issues with her husband. I need her and my granddaughter here but they are in Japan! I don't know how we will get all the stuff back here! I'm just stressed!!" says Rosemary. "You gotta just keep ya head up about that. If your faith is in the right place everything will work," says Jewels.

"Yea he's right. Optimism is always the best choice when you have no clue what the outcome will be. It's only so much you can do. Might as well have positive energy about it. We will pray for you," says Chad. Rosemary smiles. "I guess you are right. I have to stay strong! I appreciate that guys. I will see y'all around," says Rosemary. Two days past. Ding dong. "How you doing Rosemary?" asks Chad. "A1 as you would say!! My daughter got everything situated and will be back safely! Y'all's prayers worked!! I need help moving the stuff. Will you and Jewels help me?" asks Rosemary.

Chad nods "Yes". We helped her move the stuff and she gave us $100 each. Since that day, Jewels and I have been spiritually tight. A couple of weeks passed. One morning, Chad sleeps like a baby. "Damn that egg sandwich gonna be good when I get up," dreams Chad. Bedroom door slams open. "SOME MUTHAFUCKAZ IN A WHITE VAN JUST PULLED UP!!" shouts Jewels. Liquid carbon shoots out of Chad's brain. Chad uses telekinesis to open the window and exits.

Before I could move, I heard keys clanking. "FREEZE! FREEZE!! FREEZE!!! I WILL SHOOT!! I WILL SHOOT!!!" screams the cop. Behind me, I see Jewels had jumped out the window. The cop restrains and brings us to the front of the house. Man it's like 15 damn police cars out here. Smh. I see Thomas and Chase sitting on the couch in cuffs. Up walks a tall white man. "What the hell going on?!?! " says Jewels. "Oh Thomas knows exactly why we are here. We have him doing multiple drug sales to confidential informant #75. We have you on recording Thomas. Ya voice and everything. What ya got to say about that?!" asks the laughing cop.

Thomas slouches with his head down. "Man what… (smacks teeth) man I wasn't doing that," says Thomas in an infant tone. "Well what is this we have here?? " asks the cop. He's holding a bag of weed and a scale. It definitely wasn't mine. I have never had such amounts. I do not have a scale. I know it's not Jewels or Chase's; it has to be Thomas'. Chad mugs Thomas extremely hard. *I know this muthafucka not about to do this!?!?!* thinks Chad.

The cops checked all the bedrooms. They found "pocket lint" sized crumbs of weed in the corner of my dresser. "Ohhhh!! What do we have here!! Your accounting career is over buddy! Call your folks to pack up your stuff!! College is over for you!!" the cops laugh. Loud train noises go off in Chad's head. Steam is rushing out his ears. Chase is clean and is freed. Jewels heads to juvenile. Thomas and I go to county.

Chad blanks out. Flashbacks of the Middle Passage play in Chad's mind. SPLASH!! A sick slave is thrown to the great white. Visions of an innocent black woman being hung plagues Chad's mind. "NOOOO!!!! " hollers Chad. Chad is being fingerprinted and checked in. Sights of burning crosses fill Chad's mind. "We gonna beat you nigger!!!!" fades the Klansman's voice. Chad is dressed out. Chad is thrown in the hole. DOOR SLAMS!! The cold, bone-chilling room slowly turned into a mausoleum. My breath is turning into ice crystals. *Don't I get a call?* thinks Chad. Hours go by. No call, no interview, no nothing.

Moss starts growing out the wall. A crow is standing on top of a tombstone. "CAW, CAW, CAW!!" goes the crow. "HELLLLPPPPP!!!" cries Chad. Chad hears crazed inmates in the other cells. "The Wizard is coming, the wizard is coming!!! Come here!!! Come here!!! Come see what I want!!! Goodnight, goodnight, goodnight!! Redrum, Redrum, Redrum!!!" shouts an insane inmate. "Say what Jesus would do eh??

I'M LOCKED THE FUCK UP!! WHAT JESUS DO FOR ME!! SAID JESUS GONNA GET ME RIGHT!!! TELL HIM TO CALL ME!! TELL HIM WHERE I'M AT!! I-BLOCK 32449!! FUCK THAT FAGGOT BASTARD BITCH!!!" hollers a man.

Chad is holding his ears shut. The room changes into a psychiatric ward. A white stray jacket is strapped around Chad. "HELLLLPPP " pleads Chad. Dr. Loomis is looking through the cell window. "I met him 15 years ago, I was told there was nothing left. No reason. No uh, conscious. No understanding. And even the most rudimentary sense of life or death. Of good or evil. Right or wrong. I met this six-year-old child with this blank, pale, emotionless face. And the blackest eyes. The devil's eyes.

I spent eight years trying to reach him and then another seven trying to keep him locked up because I realized that what was living behind that boy's eyes was purely and simply, evil," says Dr. Loomis' fading voice. Chad falls asleep and is drug to the underworld. "Where am...am I?" says Chad. Vader stands in the corner of the room breathing through the respirator. "Join the dark side, human Chad. It is the only way out of your misery," says Darth Vader. Chad stands there for a minute. "What is the dark side?" asks Chad. I guessed it couldn't be worse than my current situation. Sssssss!! Darth Vader's mask is released. He is removing his helmet.

"What the...you...you look just like me?!" says Chad wowed. "I am your soul, human Chad. Long ago, I was incarnated in Earth's realm. I am a composite of billions of souls who led the way eons before you. I returned to establish balance and order. I am on duties served by the great mother," says Chad Vader. He puts on his mask. "I'm confused?! " says Chad. "Human senses cannot decipher the codes of the dark side. Merge with me as one to fight for justice!" says Chad Vader. The two combine as one entity and disappear...

Three days have passed by. No food. No shower. No call. Door opens. "You had a call yet?" asks a woman. I finally talked to Ma who was working to get me out. "Stay strong son!! " says Sharon. Afterwards, I am taken to a pink, waiting room. "Bruh, you good over there?" asks an unknown man. "Yea I'm straight. Just holding this shit together," says Chad. The man nods. He daps Chad up. "I'm J-Money. What you in for? " asks J-Money.

"Flaw ass roommate. Bruh had the folks kick in the door. Didn't wanna take his charge. Now I'm caught in the bear trap," replies Chad. J-Money frowns and shakes his head. We continue to talk and a guard comes to inform me I can go to population. "We got another bed in our room," says J-Money. When we got to the room, I saw three people inside. A black guy named "Trap" was in for crack. A white guy named "Buck" was in for some petty shit. An older Hispanic/white man was in for meth. J-Money was in for some bullshit too.

Most of the time, we all are talking about our experiences on the outside world. Hours and hours and hours of it. J-Money and I do a lot of talking about "real shit" and life. "Damn bruh yo' ass be tearing up this food, I don't see how you eat this shit!" says Chad. J-Money laughs. "Man I been locked up so many times, I'm immune to it," answers J-Money. He always made sure I had food and snacks. "Bruh you gotta eat something!!" says J-Money's fading voice. Days pass. "Man this shit crazy with these charges man, this fool Thomas look like he not telling them what was going on, fa real fa real," says Chad.

"Don't be surprised if bruh don't take his shit. Niggaz ain't loyal these days. Uncle Tom ass suckaz. Just stay positive man. You a good dude. Don't let that shit bother you. Hell, we getting outta here soon!!" says J-Money. Chad smiles and nods. "Hell yea bruh! We gonna get out and be on a fresh start. Failure is not an option. And you gotta get on the school tip. Stop bullshittin'!" says Chad. J-Money laughed.

A day later, I was released. I immediately had a test the next day, jumping back in the school work. As the months past, I'm still seeing undercover police cars around my house. Smh. *What is up with Thomas? I wonder if he told the folks that shit was his???* thinks Chad over and over. At the end of the summer, Chase and I move into our own apartments. I got cool with a brotha named "Jordan" from the We$t$ide of the city. He was going through court shit too, ironically, and we were new roommates.

I also saw Reo the other day, surprisingly. I had known Reo since the 6th grade back in Atlanta. He was cool with E, another person from the $outh$ide. It felt good to have some folks around who were all familiar with the streets. Plus our standards were similar, all of us being from the city. We all get involved with a student organization and give knowledge to the community. Months past. Case is over. Final verdict: Felony probation. **Thomas never told them**. SMH.

I had fought my whole life to avoid this one thing. Out of all the wild shit I could've got it for, it ended up being a fluke ass charge. My anger was so powerful it usually turned into confusion. I couldn't understand why my life kept feeling like I was getting fucked over. The court ordered 96 hours community service and 6 months intense, house arrest. This shit hell. I got a curfew of 6 p.m. every damn day! As soon as it gets 6:01, I hear the P.O. at the door. I'm in a war. Semester is going into overtime. Almost there! I gotta stay strategic. Phone rings. "Good afternoon, Officer Brewton, I have an accounting project that requires me to meet after 6. Can I attend it?" asks Chad. "No." says Officer Brewton. Hangs up.

These folks don't even care about my education!? But school supposed to be important?! Fuck that broad! I gotta sneak to the library. I only got one life to live…Months past. I finally complete community service and intense. Whew. Chad wipes his forehead. Financial constraints cost Jordan and me to get a new place. To make matters worse, the apartment is infested with roaches. And I have no bed. *Just great*, thinks Chad. I hear shit crawling in my boxes. *What the hell is that on my leg!* thinks Chad. Rent office got me bent.

While I get assigned a new place, Chase allows me to stay with him. Chase and Chandler are some laid back cats, boy! Lol. Chandler is a white boy who rolls cigar blunts. 3.5 in one gar type shit. Smh. The two weeks over there changed my life. Chase and Chandler's philosophy about life rubbed off on me dramatically. They don't allow anything to bother them. I moved in my new apartment with a clean outlook. I was on a path of organizing my own philosophy for life. I could look back on my experiences and analyze them with a clear mind. **The road to finding your soul is a lonely one**. Chase is the only person who sees it like I do.

Months passed. Graduation! All the naysayers and hataz can jump off a cliff to a pool of drunk piranhas! Damn I made it! When I was locked up, this is the only thing that kept me motivated. The work paid off. Whew. Chad wipes his head. It took a few months to plot my next move. Meanwhile, I tutor math for middle and high school kids. I share my testimony with dozens of students and they listen. I could tell they respected me *because I had actually been through something.* Many of them were in hard households. Dad on crack, Dad beating on them, homeless, shit like that.

I was overjoyed to be able to positively shine light on the kids. The black fraternities and sororities don't even give a damn about them. The campus is so divided, none of the black organizations can come together for a higher cause. Smh, niggaz. Chase and Reo join me on the campaign. The kids are so turnt up when they see us. Two girls have a powerful effect on my heart. A teen mother, Autumn, used to tell me every day about her life struggles. She may have never known, but I paid her so much attention because her faith never was broken. I admired that. Another girl, Diamoni, moves me as well. She's one of those ghetto, funny, quick-witted girls. Lol.

Those girls would never know how much they helped me. Many mornings I would wanna quit on myself because of the felony. It played on my mind too hard. Diamoni and Autumn's words soothed and gave me confidence. My heart feels clear and healthy. No rage or hate is in me. Even all the ideas of wanting to hurt Thomas have left.

Deciding to help the kids in poverty around the area was the best thing I had done in college. Months past. I think my time here is over. I have made my mark on this place. I'm a legend. I inspired a lot of lives here. Chad smiles. Some days were good, some were bad. I'm satisfied with them all. The saga must continue elsewhere….

The Midnight Mirage Presents...

Ch5 – Rise of the Khutis

Ma allowed me to move in with her to get my game plan together. I had received a Bachelor's in Accounting but a Doctorate in *life*. Most graduates are complaining about the economy being bad and all these other pessimistic reasons. I know my skills will get me a good job so I can at least save some money. Maybe I will start in that direction.

Chad searches for accounting jobs. "Accounts Receivable Clerk, college grad preferred," says the ad. Chad goes to upload his resume and fills out applications. *Bet!* thinks Chad. Question #2: "Have you ever been **convicted of, charged with, expunged of, accused of, or alleged of a felony**?" reads the question. *Damn it. I can't lie,* thinks Chad. Clicks "Yes".

Nauseous fumes perfuse the air around Chad. "BZZZZZZZ!!" goes the mosquitos. Maggots drop from the ceiling. Chad starts swatting bugs. The annoyance leaves Chad when he closes the application. Next app. "Entry-level accountant: College graduate required," reads the ad. Following question. "Have you ever been **convicted of, charged with, expunged of, accused of, or alleged of a felony**?"

Chad shakes his head. Clicks "Yes". Locusts enter the room to bother Chad. Stomach-churning stenches permeate all around the room. Chad swats and swats. "BUZZZZZZZZZ" go the locusts. Chad closes the app. The pests leave. No matter what corporation it was. No matter what position it was. Every business is asking this SAME QUESTION! Chad plays "WTF" by Big K.R.I.T. Chad thinks and thinks. Brainstorming around the felony was like jumping through a Cheerio without breaking it.

Weeks go by. I find one company who accepted my app. Few weeks past. Chad opens letter. "We are sorry but..." reads the letter. Chad throws it away immediately. Chad takes a deep breath and shakes his head. Damn this was a tough one. I had never known anyone who had been through the streets and really made it out. And if I did, they damn sure didn't go off to college and succeed. And they for double damn sure didn't do both and have a felony. Fuck it. **<u>I GOTTA BE MY HERO</u>**, thinks Chad.

Chad lights the gas and turns on "When I Was Water Whippin" by Gucci Mane. Chad is nodding. I can't let this bullshit hold me down. Man I done been through the fire and fought Hades. It was already proven life's hardships were not strong enough to stop me. Let me keep my spirit right. My heart will show me where to go. My own soul had brought me this far. I know it's not gonna let me fall off the cliff.

Weeks go by. Chad turns on YouTube. "Now remember, as above, so below, as up under, as on top, as within, as without. Those are the laws of the universe. You are nothing but the microcosm of the macrocosm! You are a small piece of the greater universe **which makes <u>YOU god</u>**! Ok? Take this scenario, if I get a bucket of water and I take a cup and dip it into the bucket, *is not the contents in the cup the same as the bucket*?! In your body is a **<u>small universe</u>**..." goes Bobby Hemmitt. Chad is nodding to himself.

"You got a lotta 'sisterhood' out here and I'm just using the term **<u>generally</u>**. I'm not using it to single out anybody in particular. I'm using the term "sisterhood" because a lot of women get together and profess this "sisterhood", when in reality they ain't nothing but lesbian occults! That's all that they is! And I'm not gonna hold it back no got damn longer! See the conscious community is a place where uh homosexuals, lesbians, crackaz, all types of mixtures to come in under the so called umbrella of "consciousness"!

I ain't got no time for that! I am down with a strict program from the honorable Marcus Garvey..." goes Sara Suten Seti. I was feeling a lot of the things my soul was leading me to hear. More and more, Chase and I would have conversations about why black people have so many problems. College showed me up front. Girls were getting their drinks spiked and raped on the regular by the so called "big-bruhs". Fuck them sick pigs. Old ass perverts prey on unaware freshmen every year like clockwork. But these the muthafuckaz that's supposed to be leading the black community!! Lol.

Fuck outta here. Then you got dumb ass white people adopting racism and don't even know why the hell they're racist. Jack ass. Pick ya head up and be a leader. Throughout my life I met dozens of real ass white people. I didn't see them on any wild shit. They got along with blacks fine and I would ride for a lot of them if they called me. Smh. This thing is about *valuing self*. How could I make this about race when my own people fucked up?! We killin' and raping each other daily. Black women have assumed the position of the white woman. Just straight got off her God-given throne.

Hell I'm not out here shaking my ass because it's hard! Them broads ain't got any felonies to where they gotta do that! Where ya integrity at? Where ya self-worth at? Oh, I forgot. The "John" last night sexed you out of it. Lol/Smh. Then these sorry ass niggaz. Impregnate the black queen, then you leave her. Coward ass pricks! Niggaz let these crackaz break them down! What happened to the Chaka Zulu in us?? The Paul Cuffy in us?? The Robert Small in us?? Smh. I'm about to hold this down and let my soul lead me.

These humans are insane in the membrane. Chad turns on "U.O.E.N.O." by Rocko. Chad nods himself to sleep. The tunes carry Chad to Amenta. *Wow!* Chad thinks. He wakes up to a sunny, beautiful day on the beach. The calm winds brush against Chad's body. *Damn this aight here! Where is everybody?* thinks Chad.

It was empty but Chad could see a woman approaching. 34DD-28-40. A tall, caramel skinned hue goddess. Tropical, lavender scents mesmerize Chad into a daze. *Man this woman don't even look real!? Damn it looks like she's coming over here!?* thinks Chad. Chad lowers his head to protect his eyes from her rich, glaring luster. "My lover, are you not glad to see me???" says the woman. Chad slowly peeks up. *Lover??* Chad thinks. "Um, I'm sorry. Do I know you??" says Chad confused.

The woman frowns and shakes her head. "These earth women have clouded my husband's mind!!" screams the hue goddess. The hue goddess places her hand on Chad's beard. "I am your heavenly wife. We were together before you left for your mission." says the hue goddess. Chad faints onto the sand. "Sweetheart, are you ok!?!?!" panics the hue goddess. Chad is holding his head. "TWEET, TWEET, TWEET!!" goes Tweety Bird.

"I have remained hidden from you on Earth so that you can fully mature. *I am your feminine half.* I watched over you for years and years. I would try to get your attention but your mind was clouded. I wept every night when I saw you in pain. When you were locked up, I made sure you had help. But now you are awake! We can re-unite! I have been waiting for this moment for eons. And you do not have to be ashamed because of your challenges. You went through those things because you had a bigger purpose. The heavenly mother sent enough ball players and rappers. She had something special just for you. With me in your heart, all of your issues will be destroyed. I will slay your enemies and anyone who hurts you. People have betrayed you and I have written their names down. You allowed love in your heart instead of revenge. For that, I owe my allegiance to you. The vampire star has sent an army to keep you down on Earth. You killed most of them with your humility. However, there are a few more you must eliminate. And after that, you are to meet your greatest foe," says the hue goddess.

Chad nods. "But how will I do that? On Earth, these humans have created capitalism and everything is about money. Nobody respects the idea that we all are fighting for the same thing. I used to think white people and racism was the reason. Part of it is, but part of it isn't. I realize that blacks have allowed the past to haunt them. Nobody can move on from their prior horrors. *They don't realize it was all to makes us super-beings.* Everybody is just lost as hell," says Chad.

"Well how does all of that make you feel?" asks the hue goddess. Chad ponders. "It pisses me off. And the funny thing is, I know I'm not the only one who feels this way. Both white and black folks know it's a fucked up ass problem but neither side can appropriately address the shit. Everybody just ignores it. Whites will always avoid it because they are afraid of how blacks will act. Blacks will always avoid it because they are afraid of themselves. It's a nasty combination baby," Chad says.

"Why don't you write about it? **_Make them feel the same way you feel_**. And just sit back and watch the responses," says the hue goddess. Chad nods. "Everything happens for a reason, my love. You have found yours. Give them a book to help them find theirs," says the fading voice of the hue goddess. ZAPPP!!

Chad finds himself back in his chair. Chad picks up a pen and pad. "Prior to the beginning, infinite pandemonium occupies all formless avenues of space…" says Chad to himself. Starts writing. Weeks pass. "Planet Earth reacts by adopting cyclical progression, or circumvolution…" writes Chad. I had so much crazy shit happen to me that it was easy to conceptualize the core concepts the readers should understand.

"Bruh that shit gonna be hard! Niggaz need to hear this real talk fa real. Ain't nobody out here keeping it real with the people. I'm working on a cartoon show and other stuff to spread the message too. We can inform folks with our art bruh. We can do it! We only got one life to live!!" says Chase on the phone. Chad nods and writes. Chad goes to visit Hazel. Chad keeps writing. Chad goes to the tombstone of Warren. "I'm out here doing this for the family granddad. Imma change life and make things better for us. I'm not gonna let you die in vain! " says Chad to the grave.

Warren and all the other souls hover over Chad to guide him. Chad still is writing and writing. Chad finishes the book. Publishers and distributors read it. Jaws drop through the floor. "Yes Chad! This is a masterpiece! We will definitely work with you to put out the book!!" says the excited publisher. Chad smiles. Copy machines print and print. Boxes and boxes are filled with books. "**Keep It Black & White**" reads the title.

Distributors release the book. Barnes and Nobles is ordering. Amazon is ordering. Kindle is ordering. Chad is going ham!! White men read it. Black men read it. White women read it. Black women read it. Mexicans read it. Africans read it. Chinese read it. All the nations of the world are reading my book!! Damn!! "Author Chad releases controversial book "Keep It Black & White" in stores everywhere…" reads Diane Sawyer.

"See, this is what we need out here! Real shit for the people!! " says a woman interviewed on the streets. "And we would like to reward the Nobel Peace Prize to New York Times bestseller author, Chad!!!!" says the announcer. The crowd claps, whistles, and cheers. Chad waves and walks up to accept the reward. "This whole thing is still so unreal. Man. I was just a kid from the $outh$ide of Atlanta who went through hard times and made it out. There were plenty of nights where I laid in my bed thinking, *Will things get better?*' I just wanted to take a leap of faith to fight for humanity. I'm only one man, but I knew my experiences could help others see life in a new light. I would like to dedicate this to my ma, brother, and sisters. They held me down when everybody quit on me. We at the top y'all…" talks Chad.

I already knew the world would jump on the bandwagon when the book got released. I'm just glad folks thinking. Maybe they will change their situation. Maybe they won't. Chad shrugs. At least I can say I did something and tried to help. Chad and Chase pull off in the Maybach. The curtains are closing. Chad falls asleep. "Chad, Chad!" says Queen Cyntoia B. Chad looks up to see a hue goddess standing over him. "It's time! Get dressed!" says Queen Cyntoia B.

Chad transforms into Chad Vader. Respirator mask is turned on. We enter a room and sit at a long table. Sengbe and Queen Lena Baker shake Chad Vader's hand. At the top, Queen Harriet Tubman gives the orders. "Chad, you are more than prepared now. Go find the vampire star's army and obliterate them! Cyntoia and Lena, I want you to send a rebel force to seek all sexual predators of Earth's lands. Sengbe, smash!" orders Queen Tubman.

"It is time for a new nightmare, my brothers and sisters," said Chad Vader. POOF!! Chad Vader creates multiple clones of galactic Sengbes. "Any unclean spirits are to be slaughtered!!" says Chad. Sengbe vanishes into space. "We know who to go get brother," say Cyntoia and Lena. The mercury star shows up to go with the two queens. "Be strong brother," says Cyntoia. Chad Vader levitates to outer space, searching for the vampire star. From afar, I see a large fleet of zombie stars. Whewwwww!! The raven and hawk star enter Chad Vader. His eyes glow green.

Chad Vader summons a cosmic Titanoboa. "Hssssssss" hisses the snake. Chad Vader points to the zombie stars. "Yessss, massssterr." says the Titanoboa. Ouch! Sengbe and the Titanoboa are ripping evil stars apart! GUSHH!! SPLAT!!! RIPP!!! Chad conjures the Undertaker and Baron Samedi. "Take these traitors to eternal nothingness!!!" yells Chad Vader. The Undertaker swings his shovel, cutting evil into pieces. "NO!!!" cry the weakling stars. Chad Vader plugs in a space stereo and plays "Sweet Robbery Pt.1" by DJ Paul throughout the celestial world. Chad Vader nods as his army cleans house.

ZIINNG!! The wolf star drops astronomical black werewolves to chase petty stars. "AHHH!!!" scream the stars. The emerald star metaphysically paralyzes all the running stars. Baron Samedi raises the revolutionary army of Toussaint L'ouverture. They drag all the racist entities to the depths of Amenta. Baron Samedi and Chad Vader laugh together. "I am going for the vampire star. Clean up the rest of these fools," orders Chad Vader. I hop onto a giant raven and fly for the vampire star's lair.

Chad Vader pulls out a red light saber. Chad Vader tears down the gates. "Reveal yourself!!" hollers Chad Vader. The chair slowly is turning around. *I could not wait to destroy him!!!* thinks Chad Vader. "What the...?! " says Chad Vader. The vampire star was a little, midget vampire. He didn't even look worth fighting. "Are you the vampire star?!?" asks Chad Vader. The old vampire looks up weak. "I am, but my real name is ego. I am sick. COUGH! " says the struggling vampire.

I was confused. "You may be wondering why I am causing so many problems. I am created from the hearts of *individuals*. The great mother sent me to test all of her creations. To ensure purity before they return to her. All must conquer ego in order to reach *ma'at*. You did not allow me to corrupt your heart and survived the tests. From you, I learned how to be happy about my life as an inferior star. Jealousy gave me cancer a long time ago and I have been dying since. I know you want to kill me and your power is too much for me to stop," says the ego star.

Chad Vader raises his light saber. "However, if you do, you are robbing all the other peoples of Earth the opportunity to save themselves. *Your tests were yours and you saved yourself.* For that, you are free. Now, **_they must save themselves_**," says the ego star. Chad Vader turns off the light saber. "I guess you are right," says Chad Vader and vanishes.

Chad wakes up and turns on I pod. "I'm authentic, real name, no gimmicks, no game, no scrimmage, I ain't playin' with you niggaz at all. My classmates they went on to be Chartered Accountants, or work with their parents; but thinking back on how they treated me, my high school reunion might be worth an appearance, make everybody have to go through security clearance, tables turn, bridges burn, you live and learn, with the ink I could murda, word to my nigga Irv, Yea, I swear shit just started clickin' dog, you know it's real when you are who you think you are," raps Drake…

Ch6 – Kether's Kiss

The book's success allowed me the freedom I always dreamed of. The money is cool, but that's not what it is about. Now that I can breathe, most of my time is spent promoting the book and spreading the message. Chad stands on the balcony of a Ritz Carlton hotel. Smh. *Man I came a long way to get here*, thinks Chad. *My life till now flashes before my eyes on repeat.* As Chad thinks, he falls into his subconscious… *Am I dreaming?* wonders Chad. *I knew I was asleep but this felt different. It's like I'm half asleep, half awake. Who is this coming up?*

A chocolate, hue woman with the head of a Doberman-Pinscher walks up to Chad. *Damn she got some beautiful skin,* thinks Chad. *Her aroma smells like honey and lemons.* "I know you are not here to harm me, sister," says Chad. "You are right, god man," says the canine goddess. She hands me a rolled up papyrus. "Mother is waiting for you," says the goddess and walks away.

Smoke enters the room and my seat turns into a boat. Galaxy gumbo floods the area, pushing my boat down shore. The clouds rotate orange and black. The moon looks like Jupiter. Down the river, I see a tall hue man with the head of a horned viper. "Sssss!!" violently hisses the hue god.

Chad calls a red and black shark-headed abyss from the waters. "I will fight you god of the underworld!!" shouts Chad. "Your soul has no fear, son of the awesome mother. You may pass, god of fairness," says the horned viper god. The boat leaves and the river evaporates. A desert scenery replaces the swamp, blowing sand everywhere. Suddenly, Chad's eyes are shut.

The Midnight Mirage Presents...

Two lady bugs fly up to Chad's shoulders to guide him. "The heart is the mind of the soul. The heart is the mind of the soul," chant the ladybugs. Chad travels for miles. I finally feel my eyes open to witness a tall door in front of me. A 300-ft. leopard-headed god stands blocking the next door. "Who are you?" asks the leopard god. "I am the son of the great mother. I am the protector of truth," replies Chad.

"You may enter, god of wisdom," says the leopard-god. The door opens and I walk to the next level. A 400-ft. cheetah-headed goddess meets me by the back door.

"Why did you not kill Thomas?" asks the cheetah-goddess. "Because justice prevails over revenge. I will not dirty my heart to retaliate at another," answers Chad. "You shall pass, god of balance," says the cheetah-goddess. I was glad I did not go at Thomas' head although I wanted to! Whew! Chad wipes his head. I walk for half a mile and approach a bronze door.

Inside a 500-ft. bear-headed god stood in front of the next door. "Why are you not mad at white people?" asks the bear-god. "Every person has an individual choice. If a white person is racist, that is their issue, not mine. The laws of the universe will do away with evil white or black people who are unworthy," says Chad.

"You are wise to stay away from drama, god of piety," replies the bear god. Finally, I reached a humongous golden door. A hue man with the head of a golden hawk waits at the door. "You are home brother. Enter for your judgment," says the hawk god. Inside, a line of people wearing all white are in single fashion. A scale stands in the middle of the room. A Doberman-headed hue god stood on one side. On the other, a gorgeous hue goddess holds a feather. POOF! *What is this in my pocket?* thinks Chad. He pulls out a heart scarab.

A white man walks up to the scales. He is dressed in a KKK uniform. He hands his heart scarab to the canine-god. As soon as it is placed on the scale, it weighs against the feather heavily. The hue goddess' eyes turn yellow and she opens a cage sitting in the back of the room. The creature from the black lagoon drags the Klansman inside the cage. "AHHHHHH!!!!" cries the Klansman. Blood shoots out the dark cage.

Chad hands his heart scarab to the canine-god. BALANCE!! The hue goddess smiles at Chad and kisses him. "You may enter, god of glory," says the hue goddess. Violet and white lights shine from behind Chad's head. A lotus fan lights up, pumping mystical elixirs through Chad's pineal gland. A bright light reveals a door to Chad, pulling him towards it. I made it!! All my life's journeys bring me to this moment!! Wowww. All the Earthlings who did not accept me, Smh/Lol. I knew their opinions of me didn't mean shit. They can't touch me. ***I'M A GOD***.

A lady bug flies up to Chad. "I recognize your voice. You helped me in the desert. Why?" asks Chad. "I am your long-lost Earthly sister. We have never been together but our souls are connected. I am one of your guardian angels," says the ladybug. "Earthly??" says Chad baffled. "Chuck knows," says the retreating ladybug. "Come back!!!!" yells Chad. Smh. Hopefully she will come back one day. A golden brick road is being made to lead me! Chad is jogging.

"Wowwwwwwwwwwwwww…" says Chad. In front was a Garden of Eden type appearance, with any and every type of wildlife existence. Cub lions run up to Chad's feet. The 600-lb. parent lions nod at Chad from the bushes. Dandelions and roses are growing at a rapid rate. SLASHHHHHH!!! "Damn that waterfall stoopid!" says Chad. Mr. Martin is walking up with 2Pac.

"What's going on young brotha. I knew you was gonna do ya thing," says Mr. Martin. Chad daps them up. "I felt your soul the whole time and knew what was up with you. I knew you were a guardian angel. Plus with the help of 2Pac, the whole hood could hear real messages as you rode around the hood. That was just some real ass shit," says Chad. DC is walking up. "Damn DC bruh. That shit was crazy. One day I saw you and a few days later you was gone man. I appreciate all the talks we had and the positive energy," says Chad. Chad starts crying.

"That's the code, young g; we all got each other in this shit. No matter if we physically together or spiritually together, ***we always together***. I'm just glad you took my death and did something with it. That shit was a sacrifice for us all, man. I was helping you out when you were in Intermediate III taking that wild ass final exam. While you were locked up. Real g'z keep it A1. The soul never dies," says DC. Warren and Hazel walk up as one soul. "That's why that music shit so hard. I was putting blood, sweat, and tears in. They thought THUG LIFE was some negative, destroying type movement. I'm just happy you got something out of my music. And took the full school route and left the streets. Hell, I been cool with the boy DC since way back. He just came home," says 2Pac.

"I knew you were coming a long time ago, Chad. I chose to make the ultimate sacrifice. It was hard at some moments. But deep in my mind, it was worth it because of the family. To give the kids the opportunity to do bigger things. And they did. That's how you got here. You hit the homerun with this one. I had my eye on you. You stayed true and I'm happy for you. Life is always gonna be larger than anything you can fathom. As long as you keep moving forward, you will always make it. Because life never stops," says Warren/Hazel.

Lula in cat form walks up with Maya. "We are glad you're holding the queens down on Earth. Always understand the role of the feminine principle. Know that we are warriors too. And all things men do that are of sexual ego, are recorded down. The queens are the key to the society for the black people. Show the men how to treat the queens and show them *who the queens really are*. Keep ma'at in your heart, god Chad," says Maya.

"And to Queen Cyntoia, we see you. We are proud of you for showing the world the boundaries the queens are willing to go to. The lion goddess is in your heart. You have been crowned the holiest tiara for your honor," says Lula the black cat. "Mother is waiting for you, Chad," says Maya. "Ok, I love all of you. I will see you soon," says Chad. Chad makes a magic carpet. ZOOOMMM!!!

Chad plays "Hold that Thought" by Gucci Mane. VRRROOOMM!! Chad swags as he flies to the galactic urethra. "It's a Kodak moment, but hold that thought," raps Gucci. Chad pulls up to the Temple of Dendera. "Wow, the whole building is made of pure gold and diamonds!!!!!" says Chad out loud. Chad enters the temple. Hieroglyphics are on the floors, walls, and ceilings. A dove floats to Chad. "What's up Chad!" says the dove. The dove morphs

Ch6 – Kether's Kiss

into Gab. Chad starts laughing. "That girl Gab!!!" shouts Chad. He hugs his sister. "Mom wants you," says Gab.

Gab leads Chad to a large open area with a long red carpet. It leads to steps and five golden holy thrones. Hazel, Ma, Laurie, Gab and the emerald star in hue form sat in the divine chairs. A hue goddess walked in the room with two cows. Chad immediately kneels. Her skin was made of cosmic starry, black milk. She's wearing a crown with a cobra tip. Cow horns come up on the side of the edges. Her eyes are like looking at Sirius. She is clothed in a gold, diamond, and ruby dress. Her hair is braided and extremely long. "Son, you are in your Christ-hood. All phenomena must reach their holy crown to return home. I am ecstatic you listened to your heart to figure out the chaos. Even I must do so. *All existence will be tested by my universal laws.* **MA'AT WILL RULE ALL**. Keep me in your heart, son," says the great mom.

Chad nods. "The vampire star will not stop. His toys and glamour are in place to test the very fabric of hueman and human's integrity. The choice is theirs. But since you have listened, the kingdom is yours. But now son, I must ask what will you do? Will you stay here or will you go back?" asks the 1st mother. Chad places his hand on his chin and thinks. "But now you are awake! We can re-unite!" says the fading voice of Chad's feminine half. Chad smiles. "I will go back, Ma. My woman is still down there. I know my future kids have a bigger purpose than I do. I gotta get myself right for them," says Chad.

"Yo' ass wasn't allowed back yet anyway!" jokes the great mother. Hazel and the others laugh. Chad chuckles shaking his head. "Keep doing your thing, sun. I love you…" says the fading voice of the great mother. Chad wakes up on the balcony. *What the…am I trippin'??* thinks Chad. Chad gets up and goes inside. Shuffling through the music playlists.

"Fuck all that, happy to be here, shit that y'all want me on, I'm the big homie, they still be tryna lil bro me dog, Like I should fall in line, like I should alert niggaz when I'm bout to drop something crazy and I say I'm the greatest of my generation, like I should be dressing different, like I should be less aggressive and pessimistic, like I should be way more nervous and less dismissive, like I should be on my best behavior and not talk my shit and do it major like the niggaz who paved the way for us, like I didn't study the game to the letter and understand that I'm not doing it the same, man I'm doing it better, like I didn't make that clearer this year, like I should feel, I don't know, guilty for sayin' that, they should put a couple more mirrors in here so I can stare at myself, these are usually just some thoughts that I would share with myself, but I thought fuck it, it's worth it to share with someone else other than Paris for once…"raps Drake.

I hope all the readers got enough info to go on with their own lives. I didn't write the book for the glitz and glamour. The fancy cover pages. The all-star reviews. I really need them to use it. I know they have things in their own lives they can use to compare and contrast my stories with. The only way this world will improve is folks got to understand how the next person _**feels**_. Maybe they will get it. Maybe they won't. Smh. Life. I guess they wanna just keep it black & white… (Drops Pen). The End. (Bows to crowd)….

*Ch7 – Fireside Chat

"48 Laws of Power" by Robert Greene is a book Chad read, which played an instrumental role for his promotions in life. Before you go out into the world, let's make sure we understand key concepts to use for future applications. We will use the book to categorize our conceptual framework....

1. "**Never outshine your master**" – In slavery, blacks were so terrified of the brutal nature of the slave masters, the genetic memory bank was ripped of its original programming. Whites used fear to create hell, and for hundreds of years, blacks are still under the "slave spell". If you are black, eliminate all of your insecurities and be truthful with yourself. Yes slavery was cutthroat, but that was *then* and this is *now*. You must re-learn who you organically are. Get into your soul and look for it.

2. "**Never put too much trust in friends, Learn how to use enemies** – Think back on Chad and Thomas. While dealing with the case, Chad should have been more proactive about liberating *himself* instead of thinking Thomas would be honest and keep it real. **Do not assume any person will do anything**. No person even knows what they will be doing in the next 5 seconds, so you for damn sure can't calculate what they will do either. Recall Chad Vader and the vampire star. Chad realized the power of the vampire star's role. He was only doing his job! Chad noticed that he could use his knowledge of the vampire star for his benefit. It also helped

Chad analyze people in his environments. It is not hard to recognize a victim of the vampire star. They are all the people caught up into themselves or some item for themselves.

Be aware of ego. This Earth reality changes by the secondly basis, making all phenomena not even **real.** Earth is nothing but a DVD on repeat! The only thing that is real is your soul and its experiences. Do not contaminate it by the illusionary gifts of the vampire star.

3. "**Conceal Your Intentions**"- White people knew what they were doing when they invaded black territories. Starvation and hopelessness gave whites no choice but to take some kind of action. Whites chose to pillage and steal versus work with the blacks. Facts are facts. Whites were successful because their true intentions were always hidden. They would have blacks thinking A when it is B. This is the "law of deception". Classic move. Always go to the nucleus of all phenomena. It is the only way to clearly analyze anything.

4. "<u>**Always say less than necessary**</u>- Sengbe already had his mind made up once his chains were free. There was no talking or asking. Only action. People who take action will always be admired in any society. Most folks are scared of action. It is easier to lip pop about what you coulda, shoulda, woulda did. Americans have been brainwashed into thinking crying for help will aid them. Everyone is waiting for a messiah. Whether it's Jesus, Barack Obama, Hitler, the American government, or any other entity. Can't no shit save you but YOU!!

5. "<u>**So much depends on your reputation – guard it with your life**</u> – The only thing you have to defend you when you are not around is your "face card". It will have records of all the shit you did or said that people can remember. The reason blacks think all whites are racist is because **of the percentage that <u>openly</u> practiced it in the past.**

Ch7 – Fireside Chat

It would be foolish to actually think all white people are KKK killers. We must remember that it is a population *within* the white community. Let's be real. We have seen whites acting like "niggaz" for a LONG time. Behind the skin, **some** whites **actually are black**, if you know what I mean. If you are white, DO NOT EVER FORGET THAT YOUR FACE CARD IS ATTACHED TO ALL THE OTHER SAVAGES FROM THE PAST. The same way how one black man with dreads represents all blacks to you. Be real with yourself.

6. "**Courting attention at all cost** – We will focus on the cons. If you are a black man, please understand the philosophy of "flossing" or "flashing" or "bragging". If we were playing spades and you had the little Joker, wouldn't it be cool to see everyone's cards to figure out who has the big one?

   Same pathology of a robber. If you like to look "cool" and flash what you have, that is not a problem. There is one exception. You WILL be targeted by jackboyz. And to be pragmatic, 9 times out of 10, somebody is gonna blow your fucking head off one day. If you work hard for a nice watch, stay alive to wear it.

7. "**Make other people come to you – use bait if necessary** – The vampire star tricked white men with the visions of gold and glory. Precious jewels and glamour. If you are white, do not think that your ancestors, or you, will NOT go unpunished for the calamity caused. Let's be reasonable here. Whites have shown over and over they are willing to punish blacks by any means. Just because you have advanced physically does not mean you advanced *spiritually*. If you have family or if you are racist or any other wicked thing, be prepared to deal with the consequences. Believe me, there will be some.

8. "**Win through your actions, never through argument** – When Chad saw the constraints put on him, he did not argue about what was right or wrong. He turned into action verbs. If you are black, stop complaining and bitching about

your position. You are only using your own energy to create a hellish life for yourself. You have had Christianity, Islam, Judasim, and all these other religions a long time now.

Let's be real. They are not doing shit for you. Any positive energy you feel from the books is nothing but your own soul trying to wake ya ass up. It's a god soul, it can get life off of anything! There is no difference from you turning up Saturday at the club and Sunday at church. The same damn energy is energizing you to do both. So quit looking for something to make you feel good and tap into your own soul.

9. **Infection: Avoid the unhappy and unlucky** – If you are a black woman, pay close attention. Your discernment these days is as good as the tissue you used this morning to wipe between your legs. **It needs to be flushed down the toilet.** Wake the fuck up. Break the habit of programming yourself to be attracted to a particular type of dude. You are suffering because you do not give the real brothaz a chance.

Remember, the vampire star uses material pleasures. If you do not keep your integrity, expect to become a sex slave. People who are pessimistic or negative will always keep you sick. If someone with the flu coughs in your face, will you get a cold? Thought so. So keep an open mind. There are a lot of good black men out here.

10. **Learn to keep people dependent on you** – This is for blacks. You do not have a government, military, land, or economic powerhouse. Whites will ALWAYS keep you dependent on them. Why the hell would they let you free when they need you to survive??

Bond with blacks in your local communities and establish something. Teach young girls and boys how to think. Turn off the fuckin' TV. Talk about family history and teach them who they are. If you are a white elitists, leave the blacks alone and stop leaching on them. If you continue, expect a military black to be born one day on some shit you could never have fathomed. Someone who would make Michael Myers blush. Choose now. The choice is yours.

11. **<u>Pose as a friend, work as a spy</u>** – The global powers that are making life hell for blacks and whites are never seen. They send spies and workers to do the job. Didn't the godfather have a hitman? If you are black, watch the so-called leaders in your community. Many are not there for your best interest.

12. **<u>Crush your enemy totally</u>** – The reason Jason Voorhees had some many movies is because none of the characters fully crushed him. Even a snake will continue to wobble when decapitated. I am not promoting violence, but you must do what you have to do.

13. **<u>Keep others in suspended terror: Cultivate an air of unpredictability</u>** – This for all people. The Illuminati or whoever you wanna call them is not even real. These are nothing but global secret societies who want all the power for themselves. I'm sorry to bust your bubble, but there just is no such thing as the devil. Trust me, if any ghouls or goblins appear on Earth, they are only going to get the assholes who need to go. If that's not you, move on. If it is, no amount of ammunition can kill a ghost. Sorry.

14. **<u>Know who you are dealing with: Do not offend the wrong person</u>** – The reason Chad was able to succeed is because he was *spiritually clean*. When you obey nature, all things work in your favor. He knew he didn't have to bother Thomas because he had spirits who would do it for him. Thomas will be forever haunted by Chad's army. So let nature work for you. We don't have to shoot and kill each other over this nonsense. The mother goddess will do away will all pests. Trust me.

15. **<u>Play a sucker to catch a sucker: Seem dumber than your mark</u>** – You would be surprised how much you can learn from humility and silence. Most people want to flaunt who they

are and boast. They will always give you red flags pointing to their insecurities. If you are black, white people will always underestimate you. Truth is they can't understand you. So use this law to your advantages. Keep a sane mind to catch all of life's signs.

16. **Concentrate your forces** – Chad was only concerned with keeping his heart pure. He didn't focus on money or women. Just his own heart. By doing so, oceans of money and women came to him. If you want something, do not divide your attention by half assing. Better to complete one objective than to partially complete three.

17. **Recreate Yourself** – If you are not thinking of new ways to be you, start. Chad's story showed us plenty of ways to move around life's obstacles. You should be using this book for the way **YOU** see life. Don't try to be Chad. Be the best you like Chad was the best Chad.

18. **Keep your hands clean** – When Chad's heart was weighed, he already knew he would pass. Why? Because he was policing his heart the whole time. When you know you are not harming yourself or others, it is easy to live. If the ground does open up and a dragon comes to destroy people, be the one to have a cup of tea with the dragon. The only people that should be running are the ones who are fucked up. If your hands are clean, act like it. Be free and enjoy life! If not, watch out for the bear trap in front of you.

19. **Enter action with boldness** – When you are bold, you create a shining aurora of confidence. Others see you as your higher, authentic self. Not as a puny wimp. People who are afraid romanticize those who are bold. They watch their every move, copying the steps they take. They love them so much, *they hate them*. Be bold and not cold.

20. **Plan all the way to the end** – Always consider all outcomes in any situation. Play devil's advocate with yourself to evaluate

all corners. Always use cosmic logic, never mundane emotion. Emotions are variable, having us happy at 3:01 and sad at 3:02. Logic is clear consciousness, breaking everything down using some sort of scientific method. So put on your lab coat!

21. **Be royal in your own fashion: Act like a king to be treated like one** – Ladies, if you dress like a hoe, expect to be treated like one. Men, if you act like a jackass, expect to be treated like one. Everything is based on *value*. No real man values a woman who seems like she is easy. Breast all out, ass shaking in videos, nude Facebook/Instagram pics. C'mon stop. Same with men, if you flexin' with cash prepare to lose it. A true boss, man or woman, values themselves and acts like it. Don't get mad at Gucci for throwing women out of cars. Hey, for him not to value her she had to not value herself first.

22. **Play to people's fantasies** – Classic method for enslaving blacks. When whites saw blacks were emotional/spiritual beings, they took advantage of it. That simple. Religions were created to stimulate their minds and lull them to sleep. They were taught to put hope in a useless object.

    Think about the confessional. **You are walking up to a human man who is talking for god.** The ending of the Wizard of Oz is another example. **The almighty wizard was some asshole behind a machine.** Think of the vampire star. **He was only a midget.** Wake the hell up people. Smh.

23. **Stir up waters to catch fish** – If you want to know if someone is real, **be real around them**. You will quickly learn that fakes hate what is real. When you talk, they will itch and scratch. Your real vibes will make them uncomfortable, forcing them to show their hand. Ahh, so you have the big Joker!!

24. **Despise the free lunch** – Nothing is free. You will always pay either something tangible or intangible. Everything has a small print in the contract. Work for your own so you know it's real.

25. **Disdain things you cannot have: Ignoring them is the best revenge** – Chad grew up in a time where kids wanted to live fast. People lost virginity at young ages and became teen parents. Many got bogged down with mediocre jobs and the illusion of fast money. No one valued delayed gratification.

    Chad stayed focused and ignored what he could not immediately have. He stayed away from pregnancies and other traps that can get you. There are 7 billion people on Earth and who knows how many are women. Women will ALWAYS be here. *Remember, you can never lose money chasing your soul but you will ALWAYS lose your soul chasing money.* Think about that.

26. **Do not go past the mark you aimed for; in victory, know when to stop** – When you have reached your goal, be glad. Don't allow ego to lead you to further grounds you did not plan for. Pride and vanity leads billions and billions of people down the road of sorrow daily. Be happy with your results. Do not value work more than efficiency.

27. **Assume Formlessness** – This is the most important of all. The number one law of the universe is ***change rules***. The ultimate controller of the cosmos doesn't give a damn whether you live or die. Times will move on. Plants will grow and children will graduate from schools regardless. Earth and its societies will not stop for any one person.

    Therefore, you must always be willing to remove yourself from your comfort zone and explore life. Be adventurous. If all you do is sit on the block and smoke weed, chances are, when the dinosaurs return, you will be doing the same thing. If you are a white supremacist, listen closely. Your time has run out. You are already aware of the ancient prophesies and the warnings it gave you. The great mother is very angry with you and is cleaning house. Assume formlessness and abandon your insidious ways. Cleanse your heart before it is too late….

Epilogue — Lyrics to Go

    I hope you enjoyed the show and thank you for taking the time to attend it. What new knowledge did you create for yourself? Did you find the hero? The character kids all over the world rush home from school to watch? The real you that drives fancy cars in your dreams? Do the pains make a little more sense?

    Can you see yourself in a new light? Do you feel the photosynthesis? Do you hear the angels singing? Do you hear the gods cheering your name? Do you see yourself as the winner? How do you feel emotionally right now? Is your comfort zone shattered? Or is it re-modeled? Do you see yourself under the gods? Or equal the gods? Do you understand your struggle now? Can you now research a little more? Can you put the pieces together for your own puzzle? Can you create your own path? Can you be accountable for yourself? Can you learn to depend on self? Can you connect back to the one self?

    Can you solve your mystery? Can you be the mystorian? Can you bypass the historian? Unorthodox, I know. I know. But why not? Why not use your imagination to better your life? Why else would all this be happening to you? Where is Hollywood really getting these movie ideas? Could it be you? Who knows? Smh. Who knows? What we do know is we have a choice. An opportunity to influence the outcomes of our questions. To be the master of our own *Midnight Mirage*....

The Midnight Mirage Presents...

Bibliography/Resources

*This is a bibliography for those ready to begin the great work. Readers desiring additional information on the "Keep It Black and White" topics can use the following guides for further study...

1. "*Biology, Second Edition*" by Robert Brooker, Eric Widmaier, Linda Graham, and Peter Stiling. (McGraw-Hill)

2. "*A History of Georgia, Second Edition*" by Kenneth Coleman, Numan Bartley, William Holmes, F.N. Boney, Phinizy Spalding, Charles Wynes. (The University of Georgia Press)

3. "*A Light In Darkness: Seven Messages to the Seven Churches Vol. 1*" by Rick Renner. (Teach All Nations)

4. "*The Book of the Dead, The Papyrus of Ani*" by E.A. Wallis Budge (1895)

5. "*Condensed Chaos, Version 1.2*" by Phil Hine (Chaos International)

6. "*The Confessions of Aleister Crowley*" by Aleister Crowley

7. "*Legends of the Gods*" by E.A. Wallis Budge (1912)

8. "*777 and Other Qabalistic Writings of Aleister Crowley* " by Aleister Crowley

9. "*Ancient Egypt The Light of the World, Vol. 1 & 2* " by Gerald Massey (1907)

10. "*The Natural Genesis, Vol. 1* " by Gerald Massey (1883)

11. "*Other Tongues, Other Flesh*" by George Hunt Williamson (1953)

12. "*Cosmic Memory*" by Rudolf Steiner

13. "*48 Laws of Power*" by Robert Green (Joost Elffers)

Shout Outz

The Great Mother, the entire cosmic fam, Sirius, the Planetary Brotherhood, Hathor, Aiwass, Grandma, Kali, the whole ATL aka Atlantis, the ancient fam, all the blacks who crossed the Middle Passage, all the hung blacks, Kemet, Ma, Chaise, Gab, Lauren, the Armour Clan, the Fleet Tribe, Taylor Rd, Clay Co, the $outh$ide, Pointe South, Mundys Mill, Statesboro, Transitions Learning Center, Morris Heights Projects, Louvale, the old house, Dad, Mountain Pass, Paliade, the snake in the garden, Mr. Sermons, Mr. Hayes, Coach Pruitt, Coach McCoy, Coach Roddy, Youth On Track, YMCA, Boys and Girls Club, Riverdale Park, basketball, Power Rangers, Honey Buns, Turkey Burgers, the subconscious, SAAB, Big Chris, Michelle, Dr. Jackson, Dr. Lynch, Dr. Buckhoff, Edie Oliff, Mr. Law, Mr. E., Mr. Martin, Three Six Mafia, Jay Z, A Tribe Called Quest, Cash Money, Biggie, Pac, Snoop, Dre, NWA, The Game, Mobb Deep, Nas, Rick Ross, Salu, Bron James, CP3, Durant, Rose, Westbrook, Lilard, Shaq, Barkley, The Jet, Reggie Miller, Spike Lee, Len Bias, Rio, Green Flag E, KC, Leland, Chase, Colbert, Ed, the RAC, Jake, Ced, Steph, John, Mrs. Owens, Rosemary, Julian, 75 South, Queen Nefertari, Melissa Ford, Tahiri, fuck it all black women, Donald Sterling (Lol), Ray Lewis, Vick, the Falcons, Rich Sherman, Tommy, AAU Basketball, Rec basketball, Coach Willingham, 12, the Obamas, Kanye, Bobby Hemmitt, Panic, Phil Valentine, Prof Griff, Dr Umar Johnson, Accounting, the IRS, Campus Crossing 301, 417 Valley Hill, 8251 Mtn Pass, 119, the devil (lol), Sara Suten Seti, Innis and Gunn, Captain Morgan Spiced Rum, Jack D, Pizza, Zaxsbys, Michael Jordan, Mike Tyson, Ali, Godzilla, Predator, Rod Serling, more beer,

The Midnight Mirage Presents...

Gas, 93, Mary Mary, Dutchmaster, CNBC, American Greed, Jim Cramer, Jon Stewart, Tosh. O, ESPN, Disney, Family Guy, Melo, Marcus Garvey, Black Panthers, Gucci Mane, Waka, Breakfast Club, Camron, R Kelly, Free Tim, Free AB, Drake, Africa, USA, Georgia, Mrs Tabitha, Diane, Chris Lundy, Dane, James, J, Dan, Deezy, Mrs. Carter, Vernon, Brittany C, E from the Boro, Ladarius, Quawn, Zack, Ayanna, SSM, 220, HitSquad, MOB23, Americans, the whole globe, white people, black people, Rod, J Spann, Justin H, Zay, Coach Scales, Terrell W, Mike C, Jasmine P, Ju, Derrick, Boo, Tyreke, EJ Swint, Stonewall Tell, Pointe South, Romar Academy, College Park Brady Gym, Nike, Snickers, Atlanta Hawks, Braves, COBA Building, Wal-Mart, Jimmy Johns, Hill Harper, the whole GSU Accounting Dept., Rob, Darrion, Kevin P, Von, D Hobbs, Lanier, Justin H, Cliff, the whole Statesboro High weight training, Coach P, Najla B, Isis, Horus, Anubis, the Christ energy, the black hole, melanin, pineal gland, the Midnight Mirage.....

About the Author

Son of the serpent goddess,
half man-half fire,
Loves his family,
From Riverdale, GA,
Loves the people,
Graduate from Georgia Southern University in
Accounting/Fraud Examination,
Took 25 years to write this book,
Loves education,
Voice for the Midnight Mirage…